*A
Harlequin
Romance*

OTHER

Harlequin Romances

by KATRINA BRITT

THE
EMERALD GARDEN

by

KATRINA BRITT

Harlequin Books

TORONTO • LONDON • NEW YORK • AMSTERDAM • SYDNEY • WINNIPEG

Original hardcover edition published in 1976
by Mills & Boon Limited

ISBN 0-373-02017-1

Harlequin edition published November 1976

Printed in Canada

I WILL LEAVE THIS HOUSE

I will leave this house, being tired of this house
And too much talk.
I will walk down to the sea, where the wind blows
The waves to chalk.
And the sand scratches like a silver mouse . . .
I will leave everything here and walk.
I do not know why grass, like stubborn leather
Whipped into strings
Should quiet the heart, why this tumultuous weather,
This salt that stings
My eyes and eyelids, should heal me altogether –
I do not know the reason for such things.
I only know that here are walls that harden
The eyes and brain;
I only know words hiss – and hurt – and pardon –
Only to hurt again;
And that the sea is peace; an emerald garden
Dripping with crystal wind and candid rain.

JOSEPH AUSLANDER
(By kind permission of Haskell House
Publishers. New York. U.S.A.)

CHAPTER ONE

IT seemed to Vinney, standing on the platform at Waterloo Station, that the train would never arrive. After the warmth of the Mediterranean sunshine, London was bleak and un-inviting. But she was home – home again after ten long years in Malta living with Aunt Phyllis and Uncle Paul Sadonis.

For quivering moments, Vinney shied away from the reason for her long exile and thought tenderly of the couple who had been like parents to her. Uncle Paul, who had held a res-ponsible post with a shipping company on the island, had died twelve months ago. Six months later Aunt Phyllis had gone – whisked away by a slight outbreak of typhoid which had struck the island ominously.

Apart from a few bequests to relatives and friends, Aunt Phyllis had bequeathed the bulk of her estate to Vinney. No one had been more surprised than Vinney, because Uncle Paul, who had been born of an English mother and a Maltese father, had a host of Maltese relatives living on the island. However, he had left the estate to his wife to dispose of as she wished. This she had done, leaving her beloved niece the Villa Rosa and a small fortune consisting mostly of property on the island.

Aunt Phyllis had been her father's sister and Vinney had loved her very much. Gradually the sound of voices roused her from her thoughts. A small, boisterous youngster around three years old was chasing his blond twin brother around her, catching at her slim, trousered legs as he did so. Fond of children, Vinney smiled down on them before they were hurriedly snatched away with a smack by a rather harassed young mother with a baby in a pram.

On this particular afternoon the majority of the travellers appeared to be young mothers who had gone to the West End to take advantage of the early spring sales. They were chatting happily together comparing notes on their purchases and juggling with their bulging shopping bags and children. The children were exploring the platform in between running in and out of the crowd. Porters were going about their duties stolidly pushing laden trolleys of luggage belonging to travellers, people who were perhaps going home like herself.

Home. The word resounded like a gong, sending uneasy vibrations through her slender frame. Vinney stood by her luggage, one of the crowd yet a person apart – a slip of a girl with honey-coloured hair scissored into a fringe across her forehead and coaxed into deep waves over her small head. Her navy and white safari style suit accentuated the long, slim trousered legs and her charming femininity. The soft white leather shoulder bag matched the beautifully cut shoes on her dainty feet.

A sunny smile lighting her delicate features dismissed for a moment the shadows lurking in her dark blue eyes as they met those of the troublesome twins who were now standing docile and obedient beside their pretty young mother. Her smile at Vinney was ruefully apologetic before she gave her attention to the bonny baby cooing delightfully in the pram.

Vinney smiled in return, envying the girl her small brood. Lovely to be married with children of your own, she thought wistfully, and pondered again uneasily on the reception awaiting her at home. There had been no one to meet her at the airport despite her cable. Not that she had expected them to. The smile faded from her face, taking with it the glow of anticipation.

Uneasy tremors again took over to bring a dryness to her throat and the threat of tears to her eyes. Recalling quiveringly her father who had meant the whole world to her, Vinney felt the past washing over her in a relentless wave – a wave that had carried her father out of her life forever. The dew of perspiration gathered on her temples and her hands clenched. Her mother would certainly not welcome her home.

"Get out of my life!" she had cried ten years ago. "I never want to see you again as long as I live!"

"Do as your mother wishes," the family doctor had advised kindly. "Go away for a time. Your mother will come round

8

eventually when her grief has subsided. You must understand, of course, that she will always blame you for what has happened. Your own wilfulness has brought on this tragedy and you will have to try to forget it and live it down."

Had she lived it down in the last ten years – that horrible day when her father had perished while rescuing her from a stormy sea? She had been eleven years old at the time. She was now twenty-one. Yet it seemed to have happened yesterday because her dreams kept the memory fresh in her mind.

Ten years ago they had been a compact little family, her parents, her sister and herself. Denise had been four years old when she had been born – Denise who had jealously resented her – Denise, her mother's darling who could do no wrong in her mother's eyes – and who had never lost an opportunity of reminding her young sister that she was her mother's favourite and always would be.

Through the years Vinney saw the truth of this. Her mother's maxim of "only the best for Denise" had hurt her unbearably, although Vinney had done her best to ignore it. So she had turned to her father for consolation. But Robert Brandon had been a captain in the Royal Navy and had been away from home for months at a time. In between leaves, he had returned home unexpectedly when repairs had to be done to his ship. This had happened on that terrible day ten years ago, and Vinney tortured herself by going through it all again in her thoughts.

It had been the beginning of the summer holidays, and Vinney and her sister were home from boarding school for the vacation. The day had begun with a heavy mist that had cleared after breakfast to reveal a sky of eye watering blue. After lunch, their mother had suggested spending the afternoon on the beach, so, clad in bathing suits and wraps, all three had tripped down the gravel path hewn out of the cliff face leading from Brown Thatch to the little cove of white sand.

They had bathed in the warm sea and sunned themselves on the beach for most of the afternoon when, around four o'clock, the weather had changed almost without warning. The sea had been as smooth as silk, the air hot and humid. Then the sky had gone leaden, adding a breathless hush, and clouds had dropped low over the water. One moment the shimmering surface had been dotted by the sails of yachts and the red mizzens of fishing boats. The next moment they were all making for the shore.

Grace Brandon had eyed the sky anxiously after waking up from a sleep to see the deserted beach and empty sea.

"There's a storm coming up," she told the girls. "We'd better make a move. I don't like the look of it."

Being thoroughly disobedient and spoiled, Denise had wanted to go into the water for a last swim. But her mother had been adamant about it – they were to gather everything up at once and follow her homewards. Denise had waited until her mother had been out of sight and then had gone into the water in spite of Vinney entreating her not to.

"Don't be a fool, Denise," she had cried. "Can't you see it's dangerous and Mummy will be angry? Do come on!"

She had gathered up the paraphernalia as she had spoken and after a while she had turned her head to see Denise some distance out in the water. The next moment Denise had flung up her arms dramatically on a cry for help, and Vinney had not hesitated. Dropping the things in her arms, she had made her way out in the now churning sea in an effort to help her ashore.

Unlike Denise, she had not been a strong swimmer then and the going was hard against the pounding waves. Sheer grit had kept her going ever on to where the bobbing head had disappeared under the water to come up again so far, far away. Denise had been under twice when Vinney reached her on a last desperate spurt.

"I'm coming!" she had gasped like someone in the throes of a nightmare. It had never occurred to Vinney that Denise could have been playing a trick on her – that she had been swimming under water to give the impression of being in distress. Her own heart had lurched as she reached the spot to find she was not there. She had heard the laughter first. Denise had surfaced behind her.

"Made you come out, didn't I?" she had taunted. "Let's go back."

Being a strong swimmer Denise had made her way back easily, leaving Vinney, already spent by extra effort to reach her, to make her way back as best she could. Vinney watched her go in despair and had gritted her teeth, determined to make it back alone. She saw Denise reach the shore and pick up some of their things before making her way homewards without a backward glance.

The water was rough now and Vinney struggled on as each breath became a knife thrust in her chest. The beach receded instead of getting nearer and she grew weaker. Twice she went under the water until blackness eventually claimed her.

She never did know all the details of what had happened. There had been a period of blackness from which she had awakened from time to time to take capsules and drinks. The only sound had been the rustle of a uniform and the worried face of a nurse bending over her. It was much later when she had learned some of the facts.

Her father, returning unexpectedly on leave while his ship had been in dock, had, on finding them out, come to look for them. He had taken a different path to the shore, a path which went by the summerhouse, with a view to finding them there. So he had not seen his wife returning. He had seen the whole incident on his way down and had run to the water, stripping off his jacket before diving in to Vinney's rescue. By this time the waves had been very high and he had been a few yards from the shore with Vinney's unconscious form when a wave had torn them apart. Vinney had been tossed ashore and her father had been hurled back into the boiling sea. His body had been washed up days later down the coast. Grace Brandon had been under sedation and Vinney was very ill too, but a greater shock was to come. Not only was her father dead – drowned while going to her rescue – but Denise had lied about the incident and had put the blame on her sister. According to Denise, Vinney had gone into the water, determined to have a last swim, leaving Denise to make her way home alone.

Vinney had tried to see her mother to explain – in vain. Grace Brandon had been fully convinced that her younger daughter had been wholly to blame for the tragedy and she refused to allow her near her. In the end Vinney had been forced to leave home and spend the rest of her school holidays with her aunt in Malta. She had fled, leaving her youth and family in her pain and misery. There had followed weeks of sleepless, restless nights when she had twisted from side to side in bed aching for her father, her home and friends, feeling sick with loss and misery.

In her young way, Vinney had thought that going away would be enough. The pain would be less acute in time, but she had reckoned without the dreams that haunted her and the lies of Denise, who had been the real culprit. Aunt Phyllis, appalled by the look of tragedy on the face of one so young, had given her all the love her mother had denied her, and Vinney was grateful for that. After that tragic summer holiday she had returned to boarding school and had spent her Christmas holidays in Malta. She did not see her mother nor Denise again. They did not communicate with each other. The break had been complete.

Vinney had left school at sixteen to look after her aunt, who had not been in the best of health, and it was not until Aunt Phyllis died five years later that she had made her decision to return home. The decision to do so had been strengthened by the fact that a young Maltese, a favourite nephew of her aunt, had been relentlessly pursuing her with marriage in mind.

Bruno Sadonis, at twenty-five, was handsome and charming with an eye for the ladies. It was no secret that he had expected a far bigger share of his Uncle Paul's estate and that he was hoping to have full control of it by marrying herself. Vinney had found it impossible to go anywhere without seeing Bruno and his relatives all lined up against her.

The train slid silently into the station to the grinding of brakes. Instantly, people sprang to life as porters opened carriage doors and called out commands. Vinney's luggage was picked up by a good-looking West Indian porter who flashed her a smile of appraisal from beneath his smart uniform hat and she followed him on to the train.

Well, this is it, she told herself grimly, taking a corner seat after seeing her luggage put on the rack above her head and tipping the porter. For good or ill, she was home. She put back her head and closed her eyes, aware of the carriage filling up, then she pushed the sounds away. She had made up her mind not to become involved with anyone in case her return home did not work out. Her fellow travellers were all strangers and did not interest her. She was too keyed up for normal conversation anyway, and gradually her mind became a blank. The railway carriage was well upholstered and heated, giving her the incentive to relax, to ease the stiffness of the muscles in her shoulders and neck. In memory, she was already wending her way through the picturesque village of Downsend, seeing again the lovely old church, the quaint hump-backed bridge over the river meandering down amid breathtaking scenery to the sea. Her dark blue eyes lit up with pleasurable anticipation, the warm peach tan of her skin was slightly flushed and her mouth curved sweetly at the thought of her home. Brown Thatch was built of solid mellowed stone walls and diamond-paned windows which reflected the crimson rays of the setting sun. The high sturdy walls surrounding it were smothered in Virginia creeper fronted by smooth velvet lawns, a sundial and paths of crazy paving wending their way between plane trees and weeping willows.

Around the back of the house were musk-scented stables where, on a soft summer evening, the perfume of roses would be thick on the air. It had broken Vinney's heart to part from her beloved pony Rufus and she thought tenderly of Aunt Phyllis, whose first gift had been a pony to replace him. Her life in Malta had been a good one, with young people of her own age around her who had included her in all the sports the island had to offer. Coming home did not mean forgetting the carefree life on the island, the horse-riding, surf-riding, swimming and dancing to the rumble of the surf with attractive males in the smart clubs along the coast. Strolling home beneath the stars in the evenings, Vinney had been kissed and had kissed lightly in return, with no serious involvements on her side. She had yet to fall deeply in love. There would be no marrying for her merely as a status symbol. The man she married would have to be someone she really loved. To her way of thinking no marriage could survive on less. But there was plenty of time at twenty-one.

She wondered if Denise had married. She was now twenty-five, so there was a distinct probability. Denise had had an eye for the males, even at fifteen. Sadly, Vinney wished that her family had communicated with her during her absence.

The train was slowing down now to a halt to deposit some of the young matrons with their children, parcels and prams. When it started again with the usual familiar jerk of released brakes, Vinney closed her eyes. When she opened her eyes again the compartment was empty except for a man seated in the far corner on the opposite side to where she was sitting. Her first glance gave her the impression of indolent length and leanness. There was an experienced look about him, emphasised by the well-cut city going suit and an air of strength and good breeding. His profile – clear-cut – was etched against the window – thick tobacco brown hair curling crisply and neatly above the immaculate collar of his shirt in the nape of his neck, a long sensitive nose and firm jaw above a smooth brown throat.

Uninterested though she was, Vinney experienced a feeling akin to excitement, a vague stirring of the pulses. He was charming, charming and dangerously attractive. As if feeling her interest he turned his head and regarded her with a cool appraisal that confused her. Her face grew hot and her chin lifted towards the window. He was a complete stranger to her, although there had been something familiar in the arrogant turn of his head. Should she know him? Ten years was a long time to be away. There would be many changes, of course, and it was difficult to imagine what kind of changes. But there would be old friends to look up, her paternal grandmother in her pretty house near to Brown Thatch, old school chums if they had not married or moved away and the two dear elderly sisters, Miss May and Miss June, who kept the village post office. She wondered what they would think of her cablegram and hoped they would be pleased.

The train was now slackening speed. Her travelling companion rose to his considerable height to present her with wide shoulders when he turned to lift his cases from the rack above his head. Then slowly, as though he had been struck by an afterthought, his dark eyes switched over to the rack above her head with a faint eyebrow lift. Without speaking a word, he moved in her direction and, reaching up long arms, swung her cases down with effortless ease.

Vinney tore her mind away from disturbing thoughts to stare up at him and find his eyes resting mockingly on her face.

His voice was very deep, very pleasant. "I don't know if you intend getting off at the next stop, but I would advise you to move to another compartment with other passengers if you are not," he said politely.

The train was sliding to a halt as he spoke and Vinney pulled herself together. Her heart was behaving in almost irrational manner and her eyes had become entangled in his cool stare. No man had affected her in this odd way before and her answer was rather disjointed.

"I happen . . . to . . . to . . . be getting off here. Downsend, isn't it?" she stammered.

"It is," he replied. "Allow me."

Striding forward, he opened the door to admit instant sounds pervading the platform outside. There was the opening and slamming of doors and a porter calling the word which set her heart racing.

"Downsend!"

Vinney was out on the platform with her cases before she was aware of having moved. Her companion was striding with his cases to the barrier at the station entrance followed by two elderly men who, along with herself, were the only passengers to alight.

Then she was alone on the little platform, a slim solitary figure looking around hopefully for familiar faces. Presently the porter, who had been collecting tickets at the barrier, ambled towards her. He was a heavily built man, an elderly man, who peered at her in the fading light beneath enquiring brows.

"Ticket, please, miss," he demanded, and stood waiting while she fumbled in her handbag.

"Hello, Mr. Post. I'm home again." Vinney gave him her ticket with a smile. "Vinney – Vinney Brandon."

The man stared for several seconds, his brow puckered thoughtfully. Then his leathery face creased into a smile.

"Well, I never! Little Vinney Brandon! I can't believe it. You were naught but a scrap of a child all eyes and golden pigtails when last I saw you." He pushed his hat on the back of his head and stared in appraisal. "You've grown into a beautiful young woman. Welcome home, miss, and I dare say the local lads are going to say the same." He picked up her cases as he spoke and ambled towards the exit. "Is anyone meeting you?"

"No . . . I mean . . . I've no idea," Vinney replied in some confusion, and smiled uncertainly at his worried frown.

They were out in the station yard now, confronting a long opulent car with the boot open. Her travelling companion was putting his cases away inside it. There was no other vehicle in sight, a fact that Vinney noticed uneasily.

The porter was saying, "It's all of six miles to Downsend, in case you've forgotten, Miss Vinney, and there doesn't seem to be anyone here to meet you. I'll ask Mr. Wentworth to give you a lift. Hi, Mr. Wentworth!"

The man immersed in the boot of his car lifted his head and looked steadily in their direction. One attractive eyebrow was lifted enquiringly as the porter raised his voice to address him.

"Will you give Miss Vinney here a lift on your way through Downsend? The house she wants is Brown Thatch, not far from the village church," Mr. Post informed him clearly.

The man did not answer right away. He left the lid of the car boot in mid-air to give her a long, cool scrutiny. Resenting this and his hesitation, Vinney stiffened. Her dark blue eyes became deep pools of animosity when they met his impersonal gaze.

Her voice slid on ice. "It won't be necessary, thanks, all the same. I can go by taxi. I wouldn't dream of troubling you," she assured him.

"No taxis,"·cut in the imperturbable porter. "All out. Gone to London to take the spastics out for the day."

Without more ado, he handed over her suitcases to the man who stowed them away in the boot before going round to open his car door for her.

Vinney, however, made no move to get in, hating the thought of sharing his car and being indebted to him. But Mr. Post had disappeared inside the station and fingers as strong as steel were urging her inside the roomy car.

It was comfortable inside with the pleasing smell of expensive leather. Her companion of the train slid in beside her, touched the starting button, switched on the heater and the car leapt into life. Once they were on the road, overhanging trees meeting overhead increased the twilight hovering around them and he switched on the car lights.

"Are you comfortable?" he asked. "There's a rug in the back if you feel the cold after the warm train."

Vinney replied on the defensive. "I'm fine, thanks. Sorry to be thrust upon you like this."

He said smoothly, "Please don't apologize. I was rather rude staring at you as I did, but I was struck by a faint resemblance to someone I know. Forgive the impertinence, but are you a relative of the Brandons?"

Vinney, hit head on by the tormenting past, turned to stare wide-eyed at his profile. "Denise Brandon is my sister," she admitted quietly. "You know her?"

He shot her a brief glance, but did not answer. He just looked, then gave his attention once more to the road.

"Yes, I do," he said at last.

She eyed him surreptitiously beneath her lashes. The enigmatic profile gave nothing away. Impulsively, Vinney asked, "You've heard about me? I mean, has Denise told you."

"A little," laconically.

She swallowed on a dry throat. A little it might be, but more than enough if she knew Denise. "How much? That I caused my father's death by being wilful and disobedient?"

"Something like that."

He tossed her a sardonic smile and Vinney turned her head away to clench her hands and bit fiercely on her lip. It was almost a relief to feel the pain. After all, what was physical pain compared with the pain of the heart? There was no reason why she should not tell this man the truth about the whole affair – but that was impossible without implicating Denise, the real culprit. She could not do that. Anyway, he was a stranger to her, wasn't he? What did it matter what he thought about her – if he did look at her with a kind of disdain? He would only be one of many. Yet it hurt far worse than she had imagined it would.

"Was it wise to return? Why did you come?" he asked.

"I wanted to come home. Is there anything wrong in that?" defensively.

"You're going to open old wounds for yourself and for others."

"Do you think I don't know that?"

Unwilling to say any more, Vinney leaned back in her seat and closed her eyes, fighting back the tears forcing their way between her lashes, terrified of them spilling over to make herself look a fool in his presence. Perhaps he was aware of her distress, her need for silence, for he said no more.

The soft purring of the engine and the softness of the luxurious upholstery cushioned her against disturbing thoughts, sounds receded, sleep was slowly claiming her, its demands strengthened by a weariness of spirit. The dream, when it came, was similar to all the others. She was calling frantically for Denise to come out of the water. Then she was calling to her to hold on. She was reliving the tragedy that haunted her all over again, recoiling from Denise's triumphant laugh because she had lured her out into the water, gasping in agony, as she struggled back to the shore, and the subsequent loss of her beloved father. The tears were streaming down her face when she awoke, to look round bewilderedly.

"It's all right, nothing to be afraid of," her companion reassured her. "You were having a nightmare, so I stopped the car. I didn't relish the idea of arriving at Brown Thatch with you screaming beside me – they might have misunderstood." He was half turned towards her, one wide shoulder propped against the car door. He had turned off the headlights and driven into a layby by a wood. In the dim glow of side and tail lights, his face was enigmatic as he drew a handkerchief from his pocket. "Better mop up," he suggested kindly. "Do you have these kind of dreams often?"

Vinney accepted the handkerchief while wiping the tears with the other hand in a childlike gesture. "I haven't had them for quite a while. Coming home must have brought them on. I'm sorry."

"Don't apologize for something you can't help," he said kindly. "Have you always had bad dreams?"

She wiped her pale cheeks and wet eyes. Her voice was low, sweet and husky. "Only since I lost my father."

"You were very fond of him?"

"He was all I had. Thanks for the handkerchief. Don't worry about me – guilty conscience, I suppose."

Her voice was not as hard as she tried to make it and he looked at her curiously.

"So you have a conscience. Like to talk about it?"

Vinney shook her head. The softening of his deep voice beckoned the tears to her throat and she began to search in her handbag for her make-up. It would never do for her family to see she had been crying. As for the man beside her, Vinney had to admit that his concern touched her very deeply. The dark eyes looking at her so intently, the rather thin-lipped mouth that charmed alarmingly and the deep brown voice so filled with concern – he was the most exciting man she had ever met. He had to be to make her so conscious of his charms at a time when life held no meaning any more. But that was all. Her former intention not to become involved with anyone during her visit home still held. They might never meet again. As things stood she would stay as long as she could bear the criticism and curious stares, then she would go away anywhere.

Tactfully he had switched on the lights and started the

car as she spread foundation and powder over her face, and with new make-up on her courage returned. When the car drew up at the gates of Brown Thatch, she was quite composed.

"Thank you so much for driving me home," she said, offering her hand. "You've been very kind and forbearing."

His sudden smile was quite startling. It transformed his whole face. He really was very attractive.

"My pleasure," he answered, taking her small hand firmly for seconds before releasing it. "I hope you have no nightmares now that you're home. Not to worry. By the way, my name is Wentworth – Nick Wentworth."

Vinney stood at the door with butterflies in her stomach and after what seemed an age it was opened by a slim woman who stood outlined by the lights from within.

"Yes? What can I do for you?" a soft voice asked politely, and Vinney trembled. Her mother had not changed in the least.

The years rolled back and she was experiencing again the old familiar uneasiness of so long ago. Her mother's cold, critical eye had always made her feel as restless and awkward as a young colt and all her movements had felt unladylike and jerky. Years ago Grace Brandon had favoured simple classic cashmere twin sets, finely woven tweed skirts set off by court shoes and pearls.

She was now wearing a peasant blouse edged in delicate embroidery. The cream tailored slacks fitted snugly around her slim waist, fastened by a soft leather belt and silver buckle. Her hair was a shining cap of dark, deep waves hugging her small head, her make-up hardly discernible in the shade of the doorway.

"Hello, Mummy, I'm Vinney. I've come home!"

She winced as her mother recoiled as from a mortal blow, dark eyes stared with a hostile expression. Her voice was clipped with disapproval.

"So you've actually come! We received your cable and hoped you would change your mind when no one came to meet you."

They looked at each other for a long moment and the old antagonism Grace Brandon felt for her daughter flared anew. It angered her to see that her daughter had grown into a lovely young woman. Her widely set dark blue eyes – so like her father's – gazed serenely from beneath delicately winged brows. Her hair was like spun gold, and her mouth – a tenderly curved mouth with a hint of an elfin smile – gave her an untouched look of innocence. She had poise too, wearing her expensive clothes with an air usually only possessed by older, elegant women. Everything about her daughter fired fresh resentment. Nothing would have made Grace Brandon admit it, but she knew that she would never forget the deep poignant appeal in the sapphire blue eyes.

For a fleeting moment she saw the poignant look replaced by one strangely like fear and she retreated inwardly to cover her bitter resentment.

"You'd better come in," she said ungraciously, and glanced down tight-lipped at the suitcases. "You can have your old room."

"Thank you." Vinney gave a nervous little laugh, feeling the burden of frightened moments lifted from her. Stupid to feel afraid because her mother had looked at her with the eyes of a stranger. But the very hardness of her greeting had made it so disturbing.

The hall was much as she remembered it, a few fine old pieces of furniture exquisitely carved and well polished, an oval gold-framed mirror reflecting a cut glass vase of gladioli and daffodils placed beneath it on an elegant hall table and the dignified sweep of the baroque staircase meandering up in grandiose style to the first floor. A glance through the open door of the lounge as Vinney made her way upstairs revealed comfortable chintz covered chairs, Spode and old Willow Pattern, ornaments of jade, ivory and wood in cabinets and books brought home by her father from his travels abroad which caused her to swallow on a lump in her throat.

Her room was not the same. It had been made into a guest room and all her old books, those she had left behind, had probably been transferred to the attic. At least it did not cause any nostalgic feelings like stepping back into the past, she thought bitterly. How often had she dreamed of this room with the old apple tree just outside her window that she used to climb when young and hide in if necessary when Denise had become a bit much with her selfish ways. Fresh covers had been put everywhere and there was a posy of flowers – a few choice snowdrops, virginal white, in a small cut glass vase by her bed on the small table.

Directly opposite to her bed a photograph of her father stared down at her from the wall. Who had put it there? – placed it in a position so that it would be the last thing she saw before going to sleep and the first thing she would see on awakening the next morning. Her mother in order to taunt her? Or Denise in one of her malicious moods? She shuddered in the cold room. The chill was more than just cold, an apprehension of things unpleasant to come. After the light airy rooms of the Villa Rosa in Malta, her surroundings were depressing and filled with too much heavy furniture. But this is home, remember, her heart taunted even while it questioned a home with no love in it.

Vinney drew in a rasping breath and began to unpack her cases with the strange feeling of foreboding slowing her movements. Her throat felt raw and parched for a cup of tea. But the house was very quiet with no sound of movement. Her unpacking was finished and a tap on her door swung her round.

It was Sandy, the housekeeper – still the same old Sandy in heavy skirt and loose cardigan, her pale sandy hair pulled back tightly into a knot at the back of her head. She entered warily to peer suspiciously between colourless eyelashes.

"A cup of tea, Miss Vinney," she said grudgingly, holding out a tray on which rested a cup of tea and biscuits on a small plate. "Dinner is at seven-thirty this evening."

Vinney hurried forward to take the tray, smiling warmly. "Sandy!" she cried. "How nice to see you again. How are you?"

"Better if you hadn't come," was the disgruntled reply, and she shuffled out of the room.

Vinney sank down on to a chair and put the tray on a small table beside her. Not exactly the fatted calf, she thought wryly, but the sight of the tea could not have pleased her more. It was very sweet, though, and she quelled a shudder, having given up sugar years ago in her drinks. Not that there had been the slightest need to slim. She was naturally slim and her weight had not varied since leaving school.

Her hips, like her small firm, pointed bust, measured thirty-four and her slim supple reflection in the mirror of the dressing table confirmed it. At the moment vital statistics did not interest her. But the tea did lift her slightly out of her depression and her natural vitality came to her aid.

A glance at the seriousness of her expression in the mirror jolted her. What on earth am I worrying about? she thought. I'm young and healthy and this is my home. I'm not guilty of causing Daddy's death. It wouldn't have happened if Denise hadn't lured me deliberately into the water. Nothing I can do will bring him back, and I have the consolation of him knowing that it wasn't my fault.

Having his picture facing me in bed is going to be a comfort to me and not a threat to a guilty conscience. All right, Sandy was surly and unpleasant, but I have a right to be here, more right than a housekeeper. At least the old dear had brought her up a cuppa whether on her own initiative or on the request of her mother. Vinney was inclined to think it was the former and not the latter.

A glance at her watch told her there was an hour or so in which to change for dinner. Thank goodness her wardrobe of clothes was smart and sophisticated and there was money to offer for her keep. The bath water was only lukewarm, but a brisk rub down after moments under the shower set her skin tingling refreshingly. She was opening her wardrobe door clad only in panties and bra when a hasty tap on her door was followed by a whirlwind entrance. And there stood Denise.

Vinney's first reaction was that her sister was not really beautiful. Striking would be more the word. The sudden impact of her presence was one of glowing beauty, for she was the kind of person who demanded attention. Her poise was

23

that of a lovely, confident woman. True, her eyes were thickly lashed, her mouth was full and sensuous, her skin exquisite, but her nose had a small bump on the bridge. The latter far from detracting from her looks added to them. Beneath the thick brown hair her face held a magnetism which to Vinney was strangely hypnotic and she spoke in a deep throaty voice.

"Well, well," she cooed in honeyed tones. "The prodigal returns having made her fortune abroad, so to speak!"

She was wearing a peach-coloured negligée showing every alluring curve and she walked to a chair to sink into it gracefully. Vinney refused one of the cigarettes she drew from a pocket and watched while her sister lighted one for herself. Wisps of smoke curled upwards scenting the air and the brown eyes narrowed upon it calculatingly.

"How did Mummy take your arrival? I take it she knows you're here?"

Vinney drew a simple white dress from the wardrobe, beautifully cut and tailored, which she slipped over her head. Waiting until her voice was not muffled by the dress, she answered evenly, "Rather well, I thought. Will you zip me up?"

Denise slid up languidly from her chair to comply, then sat down again to draw on her cigarette. Like her mother, she was dumbfounded to see what a beautiful young woman her freckled-faced little sister had turned out to be. She evidently knew how to dress too. The long-sleeved, high-necked dress with its fitting bodice and long, graceful skirt was an enchanting affair on Vinney's slender figure.

"Little Miss Innocence," she purred. "You look as pure as the driven snow in that dress – a model if ever I saw one."

Vinney looked at the slender, graceful, relaxed figure, the blood-red tips of long manicured fingers curled around the cigarette, the brown eyes pinpointed as if to conceal their expression and tried to unwind. She even managed a smile, a nice one.

"Yes, it is, thanks to Aunt Phyllis. But of course you know that," she reminded her without malice.

"But of course," murmured Denise. "And the necklace.

I suppose those are real diamonds?"

Vinney's hands trembled a little as she fastened the diamond necklace around her slim throat.

"As real as my presence in this house. Are you surprised?" she said, picking up a jar of foundation cream.

A short brittle silence followed during which Denise regarded her with hard eyes. Vinney, watching their reflection in the mirror as she massaged the cream into her face, told herself wearily that her sister had not changed. She was a closed book and one could never tell where one was with her.

"Shall we say curious? You were thrown out of the house and here you are back again. What are you, a glutton for punishment?"

The room, illuminated by the dressing table lamp, was filled with elusive shadows through which the white dress stood out palely in the mirror. Vinney had the feeling of looking at a ghost of herself, an unhappy little ghost who had drifted back into her own home uninvited and unwanted. The cruel words were sugar-coated venom, little bitter pills she had to swallow, ignoring the side effects, if her visit home was to be made bearable.

"What do you mean?" she demanded, addressing the provocative lolling figure in the mirror. Her eyes were on the long creamy throat as her sister flung back her head insolently to blow out a line of smoke.

"It's true, isn't it – or have you forgotten that you made Mummy a widow?"

Vinney caught her breath. Her face was deathly pale, waxed over by the terrible memory of the tragedy so long ago. The words dropped from her lips like pebbles dropping in a still dark pool.

"You mean we did – you and I. Daddy would be alive today had you not played one of your beastly jokes on me to lure me into the water. Why did you do it? Why did you pretend you were in difficulties?"

Denise gave a pained smile. "My dear girl, it's not the slightest use putting the blame on me. After all, I'd won medals for swimming at school. It was just like your conceit to think that you could have saved me had I been in trouble."

Vinney had turned to face her, cold in her evening dress despite its being soft jersey wool. She was torn by an inner conflict. One question was clear, could she face life at home with her sister so dead against her? She had wanted to come home with a dreadful and nostalgic longing, yet she had dreaded it too. I made a mess of things years ago, she thought drearily. I should have told everyone the truth of the tragedy. But no, I had to be noble and self-sacrificing because Denise was my mother's darling. She stood very still, her hands curled round the edge of the dressing table behind her.

Pale with anger and disgust, yet determined not to quarrel, she lifted her chin and kept her gaze steadily on the other's insolent face. In a way it made things easier to know that her sister was also her enemy. So she said,

"At least I cared enough about you to try to save your life, which was more than you would have done for me. Also, I know your guilty secret and you have nothing on me except fabricated lies which you used for your own ends. There's another thing too, that you've overlooked. Daddy knew what happened. He came down the long path from the cliff and he would have seen everything."

Unperturbed, Denise rose languidly to her feet and stretched luxuriously before strolling to the door. "Don't be so melodramatic, darling," she said. "See you at dinner."

All was quiet when Vinney made her way downstairs. There was not a sound as she paused to peep into the dining room at the polished table sparkling with crystal and silver. Dark red roses matched the red candles and table mats and the wines were arrayed out on the beautiful old sideboard. The table was laid for six people, which meant three guests besides Denise, her mother and herself. For one scared moment, Vinney wanted to bolt back to her room, to make some excuse about being too tired and ask for a snack to be sent up to her.

But that would mean putting extra work on Sandy. Besides, she could not eat every meal in her room hiding away from everyone. Anyway, why should she? She was one of the family, and she had had nothing to eat since a snack that morning and the biscuits Sandy had brought. The hollow feeling inside her could be assuaged a little by some food inside her. As she entered the lounge, her eyes were drawn to the baby grand piano. There was no one there, and she made her way over to it to sit down and run her fingers lovingly over the keys. Gently her foot pressed down the soft pedal and the lovely tones of a Chopin Nocturne filled the room. The last notes had died softly away when her mother appeared in the doorway. No smile.

"Oh, it's you," she said ungraciously. "Perhaps you'll listen to the front door bell while I go to see about dinner." She looked pointedly at Vinney's dress and turned impatiently as the telephone rang in the hall. Vinney heard her answering it in a tight cold voice. "Yes, she is here . . . She arrived not long ago. I would appreciate it if you would telephone again to-morrow. There's no time now, I have guests arriving."

Then her mother had gone, a lilac-perfumed figure, to take a last look at the evening meal in the kitchen. As usual her mother was suffering from pre-party nerves. She had always been the same. Vinney sighed. Her mother had not changed in any way, especially regarding her youngest daughter. The animosity was still there – the very air bristled with it.

The three guests were not formidable. The first to arrive were near neighbours, Charles Trevira and his son Peter. They lived in the large rambling old farmhouse which they had taken eight years before, the grounds of which adjoined Brown Thatch. Charles Trevira was a tall, handsome man in his forties, a gentleman farmer who had kept his figure by taking his share of work on the farm. Vinney liked his firm hand-clasp, and the straight look in his grey eyes.

His son Peter, in his early twenties, was thicker set with an arrogant walk, a sensual mouth but nice brown eyes. Vinney preferred the father, but was more kindly disposed to the son as she saw his reaction when Denise entered the room. He paled beneath his tan and his big hands had clenched at his sides as she glided into the room in a slinky dress of burnt orange highlighting her burnished brown hair, her orange lipstick, and the deep lustrous pools of her thickly lashed brown eyes. She was accompanied by a commanding figure in evening dress . . . Nick Wentworth.

They made a devastatingly handsome couple and Vinney felt a great compassion for Peter, whose love for Denise was on his face for all to see. But everyone was concentrating upon Denise, who seemed to be vividly amused as she looked up provocatively into Nick Wentworth's face.

"Darling," she was saying, "I want you to meet my sister Vinney."

Vinney, after noting the look of unhappiness on Peter's face, choked down an overwhelming sense of distaste at the way her sister was behaving. It was obvious that Denise knew the power she had over Peter Trevira and was glorying in it. Vinney wasted no time and came to the point, looking Nick Wentworth right into his mocking eyes.

"We've already met," she said quietly. "Mr. Wentworth very kindly gave me a lift from the station this afternoon."

Nick Wentworth's eyes roved over her, accompanied by the approval of uplifted eyebrows. Casually, he strolled over to her while an enigmatic Denise went to the sideboard to pour drinks.

"Well, well," he murmured mockingly. "For someone who's just survived a long tiring journey, you look as fresh and sweet as the early morning dew. How are you feeling?"

"Very well, thanks," coolly. "I didn't expect we would meet so soon."

He smiled. "Neither did I. Denise telephoned to ask me to make the party even."

"And you came just like that?"

He laughed softly. "I came to see you," he whispered.

Her face had the blush of a rose. "You don't expect me to believe that, surely?" she answered, and looked up to see her mother enter the room.

By the time coffee was served, Vinney felt more relaxed. During the meal her mother had carefully avoided her glances and Denise had been too busy with the men. At nine-thirty Vinney took her leave on the excuse of needing an early night after travelling all day. Her eyelids did feel heavy and she had been resisting a constant desire to yawn for the last half hour. She had enjoyed her meal – a meal excellently prepared and served under her mother's supervision as in the old days. Grace Brandon, with time on her hands left by a seafaring husband, had made up for his absence by surrounding herself with friends eager to enjoy her culinary skills. It was one way of combating loneliness, Vinney thought sadly, as she made her way across the hall to the stairs.

It was a surprise to find that her mother had not married again. Charles Trevira had seemed interested, and he would make a good match for her. If only she would marry again! It would dissolve the bitterness of her widowhood, and in time she might respond more gently to her younger daughter's affections.

Denise had surprised her too by remaining unattached for so long. It could not be for the want of suitors. Peter Trevira was obviously in love with her, and Nick Wentworth appeared to be in the picture. And Denise was wearing a ring, a large emerald, on her engagement finger. Too tired to conjecture further, Vinney hastened dragging steps to her room.

My pillow was drenched with tears the last time I slept in this bed, she told herself on remembered pain. But tears did not solve a thing. The window framed an expanse of sky lightened by scurrying grey clouds. It was cold outside and in with the chill striking at her heart. I'll never be accepted here again, Vinney thought despondently. It was a despairing thought and brought the ache of tears to her eyes.

If only one could turn back the clock and enter again into the enchanting golden days of youth where even her mother doting on Denise did not seem to matter. Wonderful days when the only thing that mattered was to fill each day with the joys of movement. When long summer days meant living in shorts with ponytail and long legs flying in all the exuberance of youth. As far as memory went money had counted for nothing in those days. There had always been plenty of food and clothes and holidays. Now times had changed. The house still had a well polished look, but nothing had been renewed.

Everything was much as it had been ten years ago. Well, at least she could help out in that direction and pay her board for a start. And with this comforting thought Vinney drifted into sleep.

CHAPTER TWO

BREAKFAST was laid in the dining room where tall windows looked out over the sea. Vinney, in a white sweater and black slacks, strolled in to find only Sandy in attendance.

"There be boiled eggs, Miss Vinney, toast in the toaster and marmalade. Neither your mother nor Miss Denise eats much breakfast," she vouchsafed, and made her way out of the room. "Ring if you want anything," was her parting shot.

Denise strolled in as Vinney was finishing her meal. She looked very attractive in riding clothes and a cinnamon cashmere sweater emphasising her firm pointed bust.

"I'm off to the hunt this morning," she said, pouring out a cup of tea. "Sorry there's no mount for you. We've only one mare now – mine. Horses cost the earth to keep these days."

Vinney folded her table napkin carefully. "I'd like to help while I'm here," she said warily. "Do you think Mummy would accept something for my keep?"

Denise nibbled a finger of toast and shrugged off handedly. "I don't see why not. How long are you staying? Depends upon the weather, I suppose."

Vinney coloured angrily. "That's a rotten thing to say! The weather doesn't enter into it, and you know it. This is my home as well as yours, and don't you forget it!"

Again Denise shrugged and drank the rest of her tea, and Vinney eyed her apprehensively. Her sister's attitude was one of bored insolence, and she should not let it rile her. Denise was Denise and she could never change. Bickering would only cause discomfort all round. Vinney knew that the past was making her feel hyper-sensitive, an emotion that had heightened with her return home. The obvious thing to do was to remain immune from snubs or irritating innuendoes from Denise and her mother.

With this in mind she said in a more friendly tone, "I don't want to quarrel, Denise. Life is too short." She contrived a quick change of topic. "I'd like a horse to ride while I'm here. Any idea where I can hire one?"

Denise put down her cup with the air of one being reasonable against her will.

"The riding school in the village will fix you up. Susan Ryder, an old school friend of yours, runs it. She married Tim Ryder, the local vet."

Vinney recalled a girl with short dark curls and merry brown eyes who, at the age of eleven, had a crush on the new young vet, ten years her senior.

She beamed with pleasurable surprise. "How nice," she exclaimed. "I'm so happy for her. I'm aching to see her again. But I must see Gran first."

"Rather you than me," Denise murmured rising to her feet. "I must be off. I've run out of cigarettes and I want to call in the village for some. I don't suppose you have any?" She looked hopefully across the table and Vinney shook her head.

"Sorry."

Sandy was in the hall when she came downstairs after breakfast. She said,

"Your mother has just gone out. She's going to the village. If you hurry you'll get a lift."

The words were growled in a granite voice emphasised by a scowl. Dear old Sandy, Vinney thought, making it out that she hated sentiment in any form when she really was a softie at heart. She smiled at the older woman affectionately and gave her an envelope containing a cheque and a note.

She said, "Will you give this to Mummy when she comes in? I'm going to Four Cedars to see Granny Brandon. And thanks, Sandy." Vinney squeezed the gnarled fingers closing on the envelope and kissed the lined cheek.

Her mother's car was disappearing down the drive when she went outside. She took the cliff road to Four Cedars, hoisting her shoulder bag in place and sniffing delicately at the delicious salty air wafting up from the sea below. It really was a beautiful world with the spring air cool and sweet heralding the promised rapture of summer. Everything was the same as ten years ago. The gulls still shrieked and wheeled overhead, the yachts still sailed like colourful butterflies on the blue water and the birds trilled in the trees. The only thing that had changed was herself. Looking back, it seemed incredible that she had survived the agony and misery of being sent away from home. Indeed, she had wished at times that they had let her die while she had been unconscious of all she had lost. But this morning the beauty of her surroundings told her that life was sweet, that it was worth all the suffering to be home again.

Four Cedars got its name from the four giant cedars on the lawns fronting her grandmother's Georgian house. Vinney recalled hot summers when they had tea on the lawns in their shade. Old Adam Green, the gardener, was still there, a little more bent, a little more slow, but hardworking and dedicated to his job. He was half hidden by the roses which were his pride and joy when she walked by noiselessly on the soft turf to the house.

"So you've come back."

The hard cultured tones were as chilly as an east wind as Rose Brandon met her in the pleasant lounge filled with the morning sun. She was a tall, slender woman, elegant and austere, with a repressive manner guaranteed to cut anyone down to size. Vinney shrank inwardly and sought in vain for some sign of softening in the coldness of her greeting. There was nothing. An implacable sternness thinned the unyielding lips and cool eyes. Mrs. Brandon's white hair, done high on her head in an impeccable chignon, was like a crown held proudly. Her cool welcome was meant in the way it was given, not because of embarrassment or a habitual cool approach to one who was practically a stranger. Vinney knew her grandmother resented her return. And who could blame her? Vinney could not.

She returned the greeting conventionally with a tender, girlish resolve to spare her grandmother any hurt and make the meeting as brief as possible. Beneath that hard façade, Vinney had a glimpse of emotions held in check and her ready sympathy was extended wholeheartedly in the knowledge that her visit had brought the whole tragic past back in force.

She knew exactly how she would feel in her grandmother's place. Yet the meeting had to take place. Her duty was to pay the old lady her respects as her granddaughter, and to ignore her would have been as hurtful as her presence was now.

A blue veined, ivory hand motioned her to a chair while she sat down in her usual place, straight-backed and unbending.

"So your Aunt Phyllis picked up a germ," she said. "My daughter was always a sentimental fool. I told her no good would come of her marrying a foreigner. She ceased to be my daughter from that day."

Vinney answered with spirit, "Aunt Phyllis was wonderfully happy with Uncle Paul. She was a dear, sweet and kind person."

Her grandmother ignored this remark and switched the conversation with the decisive tones of one used to being obeyed. "Why have you come back?" she demanded. "You won't like it here."

"Why not? This is my home."

"Because you won't fit in. You've been away too long." The fine dark blue eyes, that did not require spectacles, narrowed. "You haven't come to tell me that you're about to marry a foreigner too?"

Vinney had to smile. "Goodness, no!" She did not add that it was for precisely that reason that she had come home, to escape her Maltese suitor. She stood up, eager to end an interview that was proving painful to them both. "I won't be troubling you again, but I have something to give you before I leave. It was Aunt Phyllis's wish for me to deliver it to you personally with all her love."

Vinney opened her shoulder bag and drew out a small parcel which she gave to the old lady. Then she turned and walked to the door. When she paused to look back her grandmother was staring fixedly at a beautiful shawl, hand-embroidered with a deep silken fringe.

With her hands thrust into her pockets, Vinney left Four Cedars and went down to the beach. The coast was linked by a series of small coves backed by cliffs with endless paths leading down to the sea. The air, cool and fresh, stung her cheeks, the gulls shrieked overhead and the salt tang of the sea tasted like tears on her lips. Her thoughts were bitter – what a fool I've been! I ought never to have come back. All that poignant longing to see my home again, to wander about in all the old familiar places secure in the feeling of belonging was all a dream.

She shivered with a stab of fear, the fear familiar now since losing her father and the security of her home and friends. Aunt Phyllis had given her security and love, yet now she had gone too. Was it her destiny never to know a sense of security and belonging and . . . love? Her mind was all confused with no set aim in life. All her hopes had been raised upon the reconciliation with her family, and they had been dashed to the ground. They did not want her, not even her grandmother. She was at a dead end.

Too restless to stay long on the shore, Vinney wended her way slowly to the village. The local vet's house was on the outskirts, surrounded by fields. Old Henry Ryder had been the vet years ago. He had no family of his own and he had taken his nephew Tim to carry on after him. All the local girls had a crush on Tim, including Susan, her old school friend. Now she had hooked him, and Vinney was delighted to hear it. At least things did turn out right for some people!

The house was much as it had been in the old days apart from an annexe built to serve as a surgery and waiting room. Originally the two-storied white stone house had been a farm and the stables along with the outhouses and barns were ideal for accommodating sick animals and the riding school. As Vinney approached she was met immediately by the barking of dogs. The inhabitants of the whole kennels seemed to be thrusting themselves upon her. The young woman who was somehow entangled with the tussle to keep the dogs down was staring happily at Vinney's laughing face rosy now from the licking by frenzied tongues.

"Vinney!" she squealed delightedly. "It is you, then. Oh, you're lovely – I couldn't recognise you. I telephoned last night, did your mother tell you? Come in, do . . ."

But Vinney only caught a word here and there, for the dogs

were making a terrible din.

"Goodness!" she gasped. "Are these dogs all yours? What a welcome!"

"Two of them," answered Susan, embracing her ecstatically and drawing her into the big stone-flagged kitchen. "You're just in time for lunch."

Vinney laughed, on the verge of tears. The first warm welcome since her return was proving too much for her to take. She blushed painfully.

"I'm sorry, I forgot it was round lunch time. I'll call again," she said awkwardly.

"Of course you will. Lots and lots of time now that you're home. Won't she, Tim? You remember Vinney – Vinney Brandon?"

A hefty, fair-haired young man seated at the table rose to offer a hand and an engaging grin. "Of course." Her hand was taken and gripped firmly, then she was put in a chair at the table. The warm hospitality of the farmhouse kitchen was pervading the air with the smell of freshly baked bread. Tim was piling her plate with home-cured ham.

"Goodness!" she protested. "I'll never eat all this."

"There be more to come," a voice said darkly from the huge fireplace where a buxom elderly woman was making tea. "You always liked my apple pie, Miss Vinney, and I've baked it just for you."

Vinney stared at her disbelievingly. "But, Mrs. Shane, that was years ago, when Tim's uncle was alive. Besides, how did you know I might drop in today?"

Mrs. Shane brought the tea pot to the table. "Well now, something told me you would come – and don't say you're slimming. You could do with feeding up, by the look of you. You look a bit peaky."

Susan said stoutly, "Vinney is beautifully slim. I don't know how she managed it with all the cooking in oil that they do abroad. Eat up, there's a pet. You're going to need a lot of stamina to stand all the talking you and I are going to indulge in after lunch!"

Lunch over, Susan took Vinney to the lounge. She seated

her friend, then perched on the corner of a nearby table, eager to impart all the news. Later she asked, "How did your mother react to your return? She sounded cross on the telephone."

Sadly Vinney answered, "She's dead against me. I . . . I can feel the tension when we're together. If Daddy had died in a car crash I'm sure she would have got over it by now." She gave a slight shudder. "Sometimes I think she hates me."

"Surely not?" Susan was shocked. "I never did believe it was your fault. Now I could understand if it had been Denise . . ."

Vinney cut in, anxious to close a painful subject, "I'd like to borrow a horse, if you have one to spare."

They were on their way to the stables arm in arm when Susan said regretfully,

"I wish I'd written to you through the years – but you know what a rotten letter writer I am. I would have written to you last year when Tim and I were married if it hadn't been such a rushed affair." She sparkled. "You see, it was all arranged for my parents to go to live in Canada with my two brothers. Then quite out of the blue Tim proposed, said he couldn't bear the thought of all those miles between us. As for me, I'd always been mad about him and it broke my heart to think I might never see him again. I still can't believe it."

Vinney hugged her. "I'm so happy for you."

Susan sighed ecstatically. Swooningly she breathed, "Oh, Vinney, it's heavenly to be married to the right man. I always knew Tim was right for me, but I never thought I had a chance with him, especially as your sister Denise was always around. She went out with Tim quite a lot at one time. She's had heaps of boy-friends. Peter Trevira is still keen on her, although she dropped him years ago."

"She has a ring on her engagement finger." Vinney uttered the words unconsciously.

Susan answered laconically, "Nick Wentworth's."

She went prattling on about the riding school since they were approaching the stables. While her voice mingled with the rustling of clean straw beneath alert hooves, Vinney was thinking of a dark, wide-shouldered man who had seemed so much a friend during that ride from the station. Susan's words had written him off for ever in that capacity, she thought drearily. I shall have to keep out of his way, she told herself sternly. He holds a strange fascination for me and I could so easily fall in love with him. I, who have never been bowled over by a man before, am now dithering about my sister's fiancé.

Heads bobbed out over the bottom half of the doors of the horse boxes and a battery of large, soft velvety eyes were fixed upon them. Vinney had to be introduced to them all until Susan stopped at the last box. Here she stroked the satiny neck of a beautiful horse and planted a kiss in between the soft brown eyes. The horse whinneyed and showed his teeth in an embarrassed laugh as the lovely creatures do.

"Here you are, Vinney, meet Prince, who'll adore you. He's a lamb and very obedient. Isn't he handsome?" Susan sparkled. "He'd make a marvellous show jumper if I had the time to train him."

"He's beautiful." Vinney patted the soft nose and Prince gave her a playful push with his head.

"There, you see," exclaimed Susan. "He's fallen in love with you already. And no wonder. You're so lovely."

Vinney rode Prince back to Brown Thatch delighted to discover that he was easy to ride. There was a bridle path from the riding stables which bypassed the village and she set Prince into a canter. Wide leafy lanes beckoned and they cantered along the sun-dappled surface until Vinney glimpsed the white manor house through the trees, and slowed Prince down. It was in the process of being redecorated, for white-coated workmen were moving about on scaffolding erected in front of the imposing façade. Vinney, acting on an impulse, dismounted and tied the reins to a tree. Then she went across the lawns towards the house.

Prodding in her memory brought up a vision of the owner, a tall scholarly-looking gentleman with white hair and military bearing. Colonel Davenport Wentworth had been a retired Indian Army man and had been very touchy about children on his land. Vinney had been too afraid of him to trespass as a child. Now her dimples came into play as she enjoyed the satisfaction of doing something she had wanted to do years ago, look over the house and grounds.

The Colonel had probably passed on, since no one challenged her right to enter as she, a stranger, crossed the drive and walked up the wide stone steps towards the entrance. She was smiling impishly as she entered through the open door to find herself in a hall of considerable proportions. And there facing her was one of the finest, most grandiose staircases she had ever seen.

"Baroque, and very handsome," she said softly on bated breath and swiftly beating heart.

"I presume you mean the staircase and not me," said Nick Wentworth.

Startled, she swung round to find him right behind her. He had walked from a room to her left in the hall from which he had evidently seen her approach through the grounds. He was obviously very amused at her cautious entry and was smiling down into her flushed face with ironic appreciation.

Vinney gathered scattered wits and set them to work. She chuckled, then exclaimed, "Wentworth – of course! How silly of me not to connect you with the Colonel. You must be the Colonel's nephew, or one of them."

"That's right," coolly.

"You live here?"

"I do." His dark eyes teased. "Surely you knew?"

She said indignantly, "Of course I didn't. I've been away – remember?"

His dark brown eyes were filled with an expression she could not read. It embarrassed her. He had the air of knowing everything about her and comparing what he had heard with what he now saw.

Her rose flush deepened. "You don't believe me?"

His laugh was deep and masculine. Her heart leapt at the deep brown sound. He really was fascinating, and terribly attractive in a tantalising way. His eyes were the kind that captivated and allured. He knew his own fascination for

39

women, just as Denise knew hers for men. They were two of a kind, Vinney told herself irritably. They deserved each other and would spoil another couple. With this thought in mind, she turned on her heel to go and immediately an arm shot out. Strong fingers gripped her arm.

"Please don't go. I was only teasing." His smile was disarming. "I know you want to look over the house. Come, I'll show you around."

On the way he told her a little about himself. He was a tea planter in Sri Lanka home on leave. The Colonel, his uncle, had left him the house and he had spent most of his leave having it redecorated. Vinney, only vaguely aware of lovely Adam fireplaces and beautifully panelled walls, felt a vitality and magnetism flowing from him that was quite disturbing. His voice was like heady wine, heightening impressions, vitalising feelings. The gracious old house became an enchanted castle, and all because Nick Wentworth was showing her around.

"I was about to make tea for the workmen," he told her at the end of the tour. His mobile mouth quirked attractively. "I do it rather well – at least, the workmen say so. The house-keeper and her husband have the day off, but they've left sandwiches and fruit cake. Will you stay for tea – in the kitchen?"

He made tea in an enormous brown tea-pot for the workmen and carried it out to them on a tray loaded with cups, plates and sandwiches. Vinney heard him creating a burst of stentorian laughter at some remark he made.

Tea was over when Vinney remarked, "I agree with the workmen. You make a good cup of tea."

"Thanks." He drew cigarettes lazily from a pocket. "Cigarette?" An eyebrow lifted at her refusal. "Mind if I do?"

"Why should I?"

He lighted one for himself, drew from it and blew smoke carefully away from her. "Then it isn't smoking," he drawled.

She looked puzzled. "Smoking?"

He nodded pointedly at the cake and sandwiches that were left. Her lack of appetite had not escaped him.

"It can't be smoking putting you off your food."

40

She laughed. "I'm sorry. I wasn't hungry. I had lunch with an old school friend of mine. Actually, I went to borrow a horse and I stayed to lunch."

He raised a brow. "And last night at dinner? I'll guarantee that you had little to eat all day, yet you ate very little then."

Her face grew hot and the troubled look in her blue eyes, absent for the last half hour or so, was back in force. "I . . . I was too tired to eat last evening," she mumbled.

He said forcefully, "You'll have to do better than that when I take you out to dinner."

Vinney gasped, "I beg your pardon? I wasn't aware that we were going out to dinner."

He grinned, tilted back in his chair and eyed her flushed face mockingly.

"Forewarned is forearmed," he teased. "Have you the horse with you?"

"Yes. I tied him to one of your trees."

"Good. I'd like to see this animal that has been so favoured by the gods to seat you." He rose indolently to his graceful height and added lazily, "Shall we go?"

In the shade of the trees, Prince was sampling the grass. He ambled forward as he saw Nick take two sugar lumps from his pocket. The soft velvet nose was thrust into his hand and Nick patted the satiny neck.

"I couldn't have picked you a better mount myself," he said, as Prince, after eating the sugar, nuzzled into his shoulder.

Vinney, watching the horse's reactions, thought wryly, so he has a way with horses too. I shall have to watch out or he'll have me nuzzling in his neck. If I don't stamp on this attraction he has for me right away it could grow into an uncontrollable furnace and I shall end up by quenching it with my own tears.

Politely, she said, "Thanks for the tea and for showing me the house."

Before she could mount Prince, however, Nick had lifted her easily into the saddle.

"Come and dine with me this evening," he said. "Seventhirty."

He was looking at her in the certain way he had. She thought, he mesmerises me in some inexplicable way. He's too dynamic, too dangerous – and he belongs to Denise.

Her hands as they took up the reins were quivering from his touch. "I'm sorry."

He had a hand on the bridle. "You have another engagement?" politely.

Vinney shook her head and smiled. "No. I'm staying home."

On reaching the stables at Brown Thatch, she found a comfortable stall next to Denise's horse and covered the floor with fresh straw. Then she found some sweet-smelling hay and gave it to Prince along with a pail of fresh water from the stable yard tap.

The scent of a cigarette floated from the open lounge door as Vinney crossed the hall to the stairs.

"Vinney!" called Denise from within. "I want to talk to you."

"Later," she replied, continuing on her way upstairs. "I'm going to take a bath."

Denise was at the door of the lounge, determined not to be shaken off.

"I've a favour to ask. I'll come up with you," she insisted. "We can talk while you wash and change."

Vinney felt a tremor of uneasiness. She was not in the mood to talk to Denise, or anyone else for that matter. However, there was nothing to be done about it except listen to whatever was required of her. Reluctantly, her footsteps slowed down as a breath of perfume came up to her along with her sister.

Denise was looking her usual glamorous self in a model dress of varuna wool in chevron stripes of cream and green on a brown background. An Otto Gianz belt hugged her waist and big gypsy ear-rings drew attention to the lovely column of her white throat.

Vinney led the way into her room and went to the wardrobe for a wrap.

Denise followed and spoke amiably. "How would you like to go out to dinner this evening with Peter Trevira? I've a date with him that I don't want to keep. I don't feel up to it. I'm staying home."

Vinney looked directly at the dark brown eyes glowing with life. "No, thank you. I'm staying home too."

"Peter's good fun. Money is no object when he takes a girl out to dine," the silky tones insisted.

"No, thank you," Vinney repeated, taking off her slacks and sweater.

Denise leaned back against the closed door. "Pity, you would have enjoyed it."

Vinney put the slacks and sweater on hangers in the wardrobe and imagined Peter's disappointment on seeing the wrong sister. Her soft lips tightened and she gave the girdle around her wrap an extra tug.

"Still treating me like Cinderella," she said. "I can make my own dates, thank you." An inner voice murmured, keep your temper. She's flaunting her beauty at you, and her surplus men. Don't forget you're four years younger than she is and quite attractive yourself. She smoothed cold cream into her face and waited for the sarcasm that did not come.

For Denise was honey-sweet. "Not thinking of making a date with Nick Wentworth, by any chance? He's on holiday after being starved of female companionship for two years."

"So even I will do. Is that what you mean?"

"Well . . ." insolently, "the man is dishy enough to whet any woman's appetite. He can make you feel that you're the only woman in his life and it doesn't mean a thing."

"Really?" Vinney continued to smooth cream over her heightened colour. "Now isn't that interesting? Nice to know that one won't become too involved."

Denise watched her closely. "You like him, don't you?" she commented.

"Do you?"

"That's my business. I have his ring." She flaunted the emerald.

Vinney set down the bar of cold cream. "You might remind Peter Trevira of that when you cancel your date with him. Now, if you don't mind, I'm going to run my bath."

As she stood under the shower, it occurred to her that, if

Denise was staying in that evening, they would have to suffer each other's company. Well, there was no reason why she should not dress for the part.

Impishly, Vinney put on a long-sleeved dress of flattering fullness gathered softly from a front and back yoke. It was an enchanting border print in rich mellow Egyptian shades. She took pains with her hair and chose ear-rings to match the silk-covered bangles in an attractive shade of aqua on her arm. The colour went well with her fair hair and she trod into slate blue sandals ready to meet the challenge of Denise and her latest creation.

After adding a clean hankie to the small clutch bag, Vinney went downstairs. The quietness of the house was almost tangible – no one about and no smell of cooking. In the dining room a covered tray had a note on top. It was from Sandy: Hope you don't mind a cold meal. Your mother and Denise are out and it is also my day off. Vinney trembled and was wondering if it was meant as a snub when the door bell rang.

"Ah, I see you're ready," Nick Wentworth observed coolly.

He looked vital and challenging in evening dress. She stared nonplussed. He had never been starved of female companionship. The women had come running all his adult life. It was not hard to imagine them jostling each other for his favours. She braced herself. All right, tell him, common sense urged. Tell him that you're going to take a tray up to your room, that it's been a hard day and you're going to sit with your bare feet tucked under you and relax.

She opened her mouth to begin to find him looking down at her with that special look that made his eyes so alluring and her heart did strange things.

"I'm sorry."

She said it very gently, even managed a faint apologetic smile. But her heart was doing gymnastics and she could not go on.

His voice was deep and mocking. "Don't apologise. I'm early. You'll need your wrap," he added. "Shall we go?"

And Vinney went to fetch her wrap like a lamb. At his house she was installed among cushions on a comfortable sofa by the fireplace of blazing logs. A table lighted by candelabra in the centre was laid for two. Nick was pouring out sherry and talking in deep low tones. Vinney was dimly conscious of warmth, comfort and companionship as he left her with her drink to see his housekeeper.

They had fresh trout covered by a delicious sauce followed by spring lamb and young, fresh vegetables. She ate her portions with enjoyment.

"This is nice, isn't it?" she said, looking at the deep blue of the sky beyond tall windows.

His dark sardonic face in the flickering light of the candles was thoughtful. "You didn't want to come, did you?" he said.

"No," she admitted honestly, and smiled. "I really was going to stay in."

"Very cruel of you to leave me all alone. You bowl me over, and you're not in the least interested when I'm about to propose."

Her eyes danced with laughter. "Now you're being absurd."

"Am I?" he challenged. "Wait until dinner is over and I have you all to myself."

Their eyes met and locked. Vinney tried to tear hers away and failed. Hot colour flooded her cheeks. Steady now! Remember he's supposed to be starved for female companionship. Besides, he's given you a good meal and the least you can do is to go along with him. She sobered, her eyes lowered. She said gravely, "Thanks for making me feel welcome. However, you don't have to go to such lengths as to propose. I'm a black sheep, remember?"

"I'm partial to black sheep. I was one myself." He smiled as she looked up at him with wary blue eyes. For fleeting moments his dark face was sardonic, his eyes disillusioned. To Vinney they were more alluring, making her heart go once more out of control. He went on, "My parents were divorced while I was still at university – I was studying for the Bar. Then my father married again and I felt I couldn't take any more, so I went out to Sri Lanka because an outdoor life appealed. I never looked back."

They walked to the sofa where he piled cushions behind her.

Then he sat down beside her.

"Mind if I smoke? You wouldn't like one, I suppose?" His eyebrows lifted at her refusal. "Sensible girl. Ah, here comes the coffee."

He rose as the housekeeper entered and went forward to take the tray.

"Thanks. We've enjoyed the meal immensely." His warm smile brought a blush to the housekeeper's cheek as she relinquished the tray.

"Glad you enjoyed it, Mr. Wentworth," she answered with a smile at Vinney.

He poured out the coffee with a twinkle in his eye as the door closed quietly, leaving them alone.

"Now all we need is the music – something soft and dreamy, wouldn't you say?" He handed over her coffee, then strode to a cabinet to release the sound of music. Then he took his seat beside her, swallowed some coffee and picked up his smouldering cigarette from the ashtray. "You were saying . . .?" he prompted, tapping off the ash into the ashtray.

Vinney started. "Was I?" Her face went pale. "If you want the story of my life there's nothing to tell."

"No? You mean you don't want to tell me?"

"Yes, that's right." Pitifully, she tried to explain. "I'm rather confused at the moment. You see, the past will always be there. I . . . I can't explain it away. And I don't want to talk about it, if you don't mind."

He looked at the pain in her dark blue eyes and her air of youthful dignity enhanced her slender charm. His sudden smile was warm and friendly.

"So be it," he said disarmingly. "Let's dance."

With a lithe movement he was up and across the room to change the rhythm of the music. Vinney went meekly into his arms and they moved slowly to the waltz, and as she floated in his arms all her misery evaporated. The tune was uplifting, his arms were a haven shutting out all cares and life was suddenly a joyous thing, gay and romantic. The moon smiled in on them through the windows and Vinney wanted it to go on for ever.

He spoke first, his lips against her hair. "Lovely Vinney," he whispered. "You know I'm falling hopelessly in love with you, don't you?"

She stiffened. The dream was shattered. "You're joking. We've only just met."

"But we had to meet, didn't we? I was never more serious in my life," he said gravely putting a firm brown finger beneath her chin and forcing up her face.

An emerald ring flashed between them and she tore herself out of his arms. "I'd like to go home if you don't mind," she cried. "At once!"

Nick stared down at her. His face was grim. The next moment his eyes had hardened and he grabbed her into his arms. His kiss took her unawares. It burned through to her very soul and everything inside her responded to the passion in him. Her heart lurched and raced on, beating up a wave of tenderness so great that it became an exquisite pain. Why hold back? her heart cried. Take what the gods offer. Her thoughts were too chaotic to settle on any straight course. Kindness and love are being offered to you, her heart cried. You've been hurt and rejected; now is your chance to have your own back on Denise for what she's done to you. Then slowly out of the mad jumble of her thoughts sanity came as he released her. Happiness could not be won by any base actions, not on her part. Besides, she could be mistaking infatuation for love. She saw him standing above her, his dark hair roughly loose on his forehead, his eyes between the fringe of dark lashes gleaming in the pale bronze of his face.

She spoke through pale lips. "I wish you hadn't done that," she said. "And now I'd like to go home."

He drove her back in complete silence and deposited her at her door with a curt nod. Then he had gone. Vinney trembled but only for a moment, then she straightened and rang the bell.

Denise opened the door, thin-lipped and unsmiling. Coldly her eyes swept over her sister's slender form, narrowing as they rested on her pink lips and slightly ruffled hair beneath the white nylon scarf. To her the dark blue eyes looked luminous with tears and her lips . . . Denise froze as she let her in.

"You look upset, Vinney." Her voice was silkily smooth. "I heard the car. You lied, didn't you, when you said you were staying home this evening. You've been out with Nick, haven't you? I hope you remembered our conversation when he kissed you. He wouldn't be Nick if he hadn't."

Vinney looked her in the eye. "I was intending to stay in. I had expected to dine with you, but I came downstairs and saw the tray Sandy had left for me with a note to say you and Mummy were out."

Denise sneered, "A likely story! I suppose you're going to say that Nick arrived quite unexpectedly to pick you up."

"Yes, he did."

Denise made a contemptuous click of her tongue. "And you were all ready and glamorous. Pull the other leg – it's got bells on! Mummy wants to see you. She's in the lounge."

Grace Brandon was seated on the sofa by the fireplace, a glass of sherry in her hand. She wore a black woollen dress with a silver ornament which matched the silver belt, and her look was impersonal. It seemed incredible to Vinny that, after years of separation and the weariness of travel, there was no welcome for her in the cold brown eyes.

"Sit down, Vinney," her mother commanded.

Vinney sat down in a chair under a wall light which turned her hair into spun gold. She was relieved that her mother had spoken first, for she could think of nothing to say. Denise was taking a cigarette from the silver box on a table and flicked a matching silver table light into flame. Vinney recognised them as gifts from her father, two of the many things he had brought home for her mother from time to time. They seemed to wink at her in the light and she took comfort from them.

Denise lounged in a chair gracefully. "My charming sister has been out with Nick after telling me that she was staying home this evening, Mummy. What do you think about that for being crafty?" she said tartly.

Her mother showed no great surprise. "Since you weren't available, I'm not surprised." Her eyes strayed to her younger daughter who was folding the white nylon scarf on her knee.

There was an untouched air of sweetness about her, in marked contrast to Denise's hard sophistication. Her dress was very pretty too, Grace admitted to herself reluctantly, and spoke her thoughts aloud. "It seems you have a rival."

Denise was suddenly waspish. "You could be right, Mummy. What did you come home for, darling," sarcastically, "to find a husband?"

Vinney refused to shrink at the venom in her voice. It was several seconds before she answered in a voice as smooth as cream. "That isn't very likely, is it, since you're now twenty-five and still unmarried. The outlook is pretty bleak for me, wouldn't you say?"

"Why, you little . . . !" Denise spat out furiously as her mother cut in.

"No bickering between you two. I won't have it, and I won't have Denise upset, Vinney. Understand?" She regarded her younger daughter with hard eyes. "Please remember that you are only a guest in this house."

Vinney did shrink a little now, shattered by her mother's words. So she was to be regarded as a guest, a paying guest, since her mother had accepted the money she had left with Sandy without a word. Tears blocked her throat, but pride came to her aid at the smug look on her sister's face.

"I'm not likely to be allowed to forget it, am I?" she replied bitterly. "And now I'll go to bed, if you don't mind."

"You will hear what I have to say first." Grace Brandon looked down into her sherry. "You've been invited to the Hunt Ball which is being held at Charles Trevira's house because the town hall is being modernised. I've been there this evening to help with the arrangements. I shall expect you to accept, since everyone of importance will be there!"

Vinney rose to her feet. She felt numb and terribly depressed. A sudden urge to rush upstairs and pack her cases washed over her. Her mother was drinking her sherry and Denise was at the sideboard pouring out a nightcap for herself. She hesitated for a moment as the tension of the past few days mounted inside her. I was determined not to be hurt or upset at anything yet here I am ready to burst into tears and run away

49

like the coward I am, she thought. In that moment she knew the real reason why she had to come home. It was to rid herself of the nightmares of guilt and anguish that were ruining her life. Only by returning to the scene of the tragedy could she purge herself of her torture. Don't be a coward, girl, a small voice hissed in an obscure corner of her mind. You don't have to become involved emotionally with people who don't care a jot for you. Your father loved you and he died the way he would have wanted to die, in his beloved sea. And it was not your fault.

With her chin lifted Vinney walked quietly from the room after a murmured goodnight. They might have offered her a drink and been sociable, those two strangers who were her mother and sister.

CHAPTER THREE

AFTER a surprisingly good night through which she had slept dreamlessly, Vinney awakened to a rosy, sparkling morning. Spring was always a heartening experience in spite of pressing problems and she was glad now that she had come home. It had to be, just as it had to be her problem and no one else's. Her father's portrait on the wall of her room caught her eye more than once as she tidied her room. Hurt and unhappy though she was, and determined to avoid further emotional scenes with her family, there was a certain amount of comfort to be found in looking at his serene countenance. His presence in the house was almost tangible.

She began to feel cheerful on her way downstairs to breakfast, but her cheerfulness was dimmed by the fact that neither her mother nor Denise put in an appearance during her meal. Vinney did not eat much, but she drank her coffee thirstily, determined not to be hurt by the deliberate snub of leaving her on her own. They still had not put in an appearance when she went to the kitchen to give Sandy an envelope containing money towards Prince's keep.

"For Denise when she comes down," she said, giving it to Sandy with a smile.

Vinney had decided to ride to the village on Prince and leave him at the riding school while she made an appointment at the village hairdressers and did a little shopping. She wasn't looking forward to going to the Hunt ball. As her mother had said, everyone would be there with herself as the only stranger in their midst. They would stare curiously at the prodigal daughter and the whole tragic incident of ten years ago would be rehashed and chewed over with enjoyment. There I go again, she thought, worrying about the opinions of people who don't really matter.

Prince was easy to ride, being free from moods and sensing her need to get away from it all. He cantered along on a small whinney of pleasure and slowed down as they neared Nick Wentworth's estate.

"Not today, darling." Vinney leaned forward to pat the satiny neck. "We're going to the village."

After a swift glance through the trees at the house, she urged Prince on. In some strange way she felt an affinity with Nick Wentworth, an affinity that remained unresolved whenever she thought of him. It would be so easy to fall in love with him, and the memory of his kiss brought a blush to her cheeks. It was wrong for her to think about him, since he belonged to Denise. Why had she not challenged him with it? Because I'm a coward. I couldn't bear to hear him admit it, she told herself miserably.

Susan was in the paddock at the stables putting mounted youngsters through their paces. She nodded when Vinney asked permission to leave Prince while she went shopping, and her smile was heartwarming. The hairdressers was a rather smart establishment with a deep mauve carpet and silver fittings. A small, dapper young man with a Latin look was talking to the receptionist as he wrote something in the appointment book when she entered.

When Vinney asked for an appointment on the day of the Hunt Ball she was told that they were fully booked for that day. However, the young man, Antonio by name and obviously the owner of the name over the window, conferred with the receptionist, then gave Vinney a dazzling smile. She would be sandwiched in between two more customers, he said, to the surprise of the girl who booked it down. Heartened by this and by the look of appraisal in Antonio's dark eyes, Vinney asked if there was any chance of a shampoo and set that morning. Again the brilliant smile. If Madam did not mind waiting for a little while, he would attend to her personally. And he did.

"You obviously have something no one else has," the pert miss at the cash desk told her when she paid her bill. "I've never known Antonio to do that before for a complete stranger. Perhaps you're an old friend of his. That would explain it."

Vinney, unable to give any explanation for the VIP treatment, shook her head and admitted honestly, "I only arrived in this country yesterday. I've never seen Antonio before."

The girl looked disdainfully down her nose. "Some folks have all the luck! Perhaps you'll buy a draw ticket for the spastics' annual draw – first prize a car. You're the kind who will probably win it."

She pushed a book of tickets under Vinney's nose and flicked slightly protruding, pale blue eyes on the beautifully tailored riding outfit gracing her slender form. Her expression defied refusal.

"Keep the change." Vinney paid generously for the whole book and filled in her name and address quickly on each ticket, then left quickly to escape further curious stares.

The post office was next door and a slender person with a sweet smile emerged from the shadows behind the counter to serve her.

Vinney greeted her with a dimpled smile. "Hello, Miss May. I'm Vinney, Vinney Brandon."

Miss May's eyes widened to their full extent and she beamed with delight.

"Well, I never! How pretty you've grown. Quite a young lady."

"I'm twenty-one," Vinney smiled. "How is Miss June?"

Miss June came hurriedly into the shop then from the living quarters, having heard her sister's cry of surprise. The sisters were very much alike. Both were small and delicately boned, with small elfin faces and Alice bands around their white, curly hair. Vinney had never known them to be any different from what they were now, elderly and kind. Apart from being a little more frail they had not changed. They were genuinely pleased to see her and they insisted on her having a cup of tea with them.

It was while she was enjoying a cup of tea and catching up with the news of the last ten years that the skies darkened and a deluge of rain spattered the latticed window of the pretty room. Later, when she left with their good wishes ringing in her ears, Vinney found the gutters below the kerb overflowing with water which had come down too quickly for the drains to absorb it immediately. The rain had stopped and a watery sun was pushing its way through the opening clouds. After a visit to the pharmacy and the bookshop Vinney decided to lunch out, and stood on the kerb for a large van to pass before crossing the road.

She was blissfully unaware of the car following the van until the shrieking of brakes rent the air piercingly. Startled, she stepped back, twisted towards the kerb and lost her balance. The car passed very close, tyres screeched, the engine was shut off and the car door slammed. Vinney shuddered. The water in the gutter was cold and she had fallen into it very painfully on her left elbow. Dazed and shocked, she scrambled to her feet and looked around for her parcels.

The driver of the car was striding towards her furious and arrogant and she looked up into the face of Nick Wentworth.

"What the hell . . ." he began, than stopped in astonishment. "Vinney? What are you trying to do, commit suicide? Are you hurt?"

Ignoring the small crowd closing in on the scene, he reached out and drew her shaking form against him. She clung to him for a moment feeling rather sick.

"I . . . I'm awfully sorry. I didn't see you," she confessed on a small sob of relief.

"You little idiot!" Anger flowed from him and he said sharply, "You might have been killed." His hands moved over her probingly. "Are you sure I didn't hit you at all?"

"Yes, I'm sure."

He watched her exasperatedly as she put a hand to her hair soaked down one side where her head had hit the ground. Apparently he was as shaken as she was, for his anger increased. Her shoulders were gripped in fingers of steel and he glared down into her white face.

"You have no pain anywhere?" he demanded.

She straightened painfully and ignored the throbbing in her elbow. Her hands were shaking and she tried to steady them by smoothing her jacket down.

"You didn't even touch me," she said through pale lips. "I'm very sorry for being so careless."

His anger evaporated on a sigh of relief and there was a

slight pause while his eyes raked her face. What he saw there did not apparently entirely convince him that she had escaped so lightly, for he did not smile but said grimly, "Come on, I'll take you home. You are alone?"

He asked the last question as he released her to scoop up her purchases scattered around in the wet. Miserably Vinney answered in the affirmative and hastily wiped her hands on her handkerchief. Her legs were like jelly and she was grateful for his support to the car.

The plastic shopping bag containing her goods was put on the back seat and Nick put her in front. The trembling in her legs continued through her whole being as he went rapidly around to slide in beside her in the driving seat, and she began to laugh hysterically.

"It really is funny," she gasped, aware of his startled look. "I've had a shampoo and set at the hairdressers this morning – and look at me! I look as if I'd been drawn through a hedge backwards."

"I'm looking," he told her gravely. "You need a hot bath when you get home and a warm, sweet drink to counteract the sense of shock."

He started the car and shot another startled glance at her when she grabbed his arm. "I forgot – I've left Prince at the riding stables. I'll be grateful if you'll take me there. I can ride home then."

She managed a smile, but he gave no answering one. Instead he set off at speed and was soon passing the riding school.

"Prince can wait," he said with his eyes on the road. "I'll ride him over for you later."

Vinney bit on a trembling lip. "I don't want you to ride him over for me," she protested on a husky whisper. "And I don't want you to drive me home like this either. The last thing I want is to give my family any cause to complain about me. In any case . . ." Here her voice broke and for several moments it was impossible for her to go on. "Don't you see I've given them enough trouble already?" Her lips were trembling now uncontrollably, and her tone sharpened. "I . . . I demand to be taken back to the riding stables for Prince. I'm all right now."

"Relax and stop worrying." He spoke as one would do to a child and he shot a look at her small face now so tragically pale that he frowned irritably, although his voice was suddenly very gentle. "It's not the end of the world, you know. Relax, there's a good girl. We'll soon have you warm and dry."

His dark eyes mocked her wretched ones and Vinney found herself crying quietly.

He let her cry for about a minute then, "Vinney?" Beneath the curt command there was an underlying tenderness.

She dabbed furiously at her eyes and gulped. "Yes?"

"Stop it before I beat you and give you something to cry about. Do you hear me?"

He reached for his handkerchief with one hand and gave it to her without turning his head. Vinney mumbled her thanks, and gradually the storm of tears abated, leaving unhappiness forming like ice on the waves of her sea of distress. Confusion went through her like a searing pain. I've made myself look a fool in front of Nick Wentworth of all people. Why did it have to be him? she asked herself despairingly. It was no use trying to convince herself that other people's opinion of her did not matter. Nick Wentworth's did, enormously.

To her dismay the car turned into the driveway of his house and he was out in a trice to open her door.

"The lesser of the two evils," he said laconically. "Come on."

Meekly, Vinney allowed him to help her from the car. Her wet jacket stuck clammy and cold to her skin and her elbow throbbed painfully. He noticed her wince when his fingers curled around it and he hustled her grimly into the house.

"Mrs. Blake!" he thundered in the hall and, as that good lady appeared, he continued, "Will you run a hot bath and find a warm wrap for Miss Brandon? She's had a fall and her clothes are wet."

Mrs. Blake, a plump, motherly person, looked distressed. "Dear me!" she exclaimed. "Shall I telephone for the doctor?"

"No, thanks." Nick threw the words over his shoulder as he piloted Vinney to the lounge. "But be quick about the bath, there's a dear."

56

A log fire crackled merrily in the fireplace and, as Nick released her arm, a sick feeling became more acute in her stomach. At the same moment he moved from her side across the room and she could see him pouring brandy from a bottle on the sideboard.

"Sit down by the fire," he commanded in the same clipped tones. Unhappy and tense, Vinney obeyed, and he came to her with the brandy. "Drink this – all of it," he ordered. "Then you can take a bath and lunch with me while your clothes are drying."

After several sips from the glass the colour gradually returned to her face and her cheeks were burning beneath his scrutiny when she returned the empty glass. Tenderly he helped her off with her jacket to lift the sodden sleeve of the shirt underneath where it had stuck to her injured elbow. Vinney hardly felt him ease the fabric away from the bruise, so gentle were his fingers, and she eyed him covertly as he rolled up her sleeve and bent his head sideways to look at the injured place.

Again she was aware that the sheer virility of the man had a dominant quality about it, a quality far more fundamental than mere charm. She knew that, as a rule, big, strong men were not infrequently blessed with a gentle nature, yet she was sure that gentleness was only a very minor part of Nick Wentworth's make-up. There was nothing weak or indecisive about him. First and foremost he was the all-conquering male with that lazy charm of his conveying a sense of mastery emphasised by each deliberate movement. And because her thoughts were subconsciously dwelling upon her sister Denise, Vinney hardened herself against his charm.

He said, "Apart from the skin being broken no great harm has been done. You probably fell heavily on your side, hence the bruised elbow." He lowered her arm and captured her eyes with his own. Absurd that his voice should play on her heart-strings so acutely, stirring them into song. "No doubt it will sting when you're in the bath, but the water will do it good. I'll put an adhesive dressing on it afterwards."

Vinney did not reply – there was nothing to say – she was

beyond words. She hadn't a clue to why he should disturb her so much, and it was a relief when Mrs. Blake came into the room to say that the bath water was running nice and hot and that everything was ready.

Twenty minutes later she was back in the lounge clad in a pair of Mrs. Blake's pyjamas and her voluminous dressing gown wound almost twice around her slim form and tied with a girdle.

Nick was smiling, a twinkling, mirthful smile which eased the tension inside her.

"So the admirable Mrs. Blake has fixed you up," he said with approval. "Your clothes shouldn't be long drying since you weren't completely soaked. I hope it's whetted your appetite – or does that sound trite?"

Vinney smiled. "It . . . it sounds nice and friendly. I'm very grateful to you." She laughed nervously to fill in the pause. There was no mirth in it. "It seems I'm always dining here. This is the third time. Do you know that?"

"I know I had every intention of making your acquaintance, so what better than over a meal?" he returned bluntly.

"I agree." For some reason Vinney felt suddenly light-hearted. "But supposing" – smiling – "I can't return the compliment and ask you to my home in return?" A strange gleam in his eyes made her lower her own quickly, and she added, "I'm sorry. I'm sure you understand."

"There's nothing to understand," he replied forcefully. "I usually have things my way when I want them."

"But friendship is give and take," she protested. "It can't possibly exist on just taking. Not for me it can't."

His eyes gleamed again, this time with devilment as he put an arm carelessly around her shoulders. "You're too intense, my child. Who said anything about friendship? Let's eat."

Over lunch the tension evaporated and the conversation was taken into more impersonal channels. He talked about his job in Sri Lanka, of the lovely house set in the wooded hills looking out on magnificent scenery and his friend, a Scot, elderly, aged sixty to be exact, just twice his age.

He grinned. "Good old Mac," he said. "Doesn't look any

older than I do." His eyes twinkled. "Perhaps because he hasn't been married."

Unobtrusively, he had seen that she was constantly supplied with all the good things on the table and, as with home cooking, there was far too much of everything. Now, replete with a good meal and feeling mellowed by the delicious coffee, Vinney felt almost carefree and happy.

"Is that why you've remained a bachelor for so long, because you're against marriage?" she queried.

There was an element of self-mockery in the brief smile that flickered over Nick's face.

"No," he answered. "I've no little woman living with me either. Are you surprised?"

"Why should I be?" – lightly. "I've never given it a thought."

"Would it have mattered to you if I had?" he asked quietly.

The gleam was more pronounced in his eyes and Vinney wished he would not look at her so intently. She was suddenly aware that it was on the cards for her to be a little afraid of the masterful side of him which he was taking no pains to conceal.

"It's none of my business, is it?" she answered quickly. It seemed that she was defying some threatened trouble beyond her control.

"Perhaps not," he conceded. "More coffee?"

She shook her head and her lighthearted mood burst like the bubble it was. She wanted to cry because he had believed her pretended indifference to him so readily. They sat in uncomfortable silence. Vinney was thinking about Denise and the emerald ring which bound her to Nick. Not for anything could she have mentioned her sister's name or the ring.

The conversation that eventually followed was spasmodic, for neither had much to say. It was a relief to them both when Mrs. Blake came in to say that Miss Brandon's things were now dry and had been pressed, if she cared to go to the warm kitchen to put them on.

"That's a painful bruise on your elbow, my dear," Mrs. Blake exclaimed sympathetically as she helped Vinney on with the soft silk shirt over her bra and riding breeches. "Where's the first aid box? I'll put you a dressing on it." She went to the cupboard in the kitchen recess, opened it and put her hand inside. "The first aid box isn't here," she said. "Mr. Wentworth must have it. He must have fetched it while you were in the bath. Better leave your shirt unbuttoned until he's dressed the wound."

Nick made short work of applying an adhesive dressing to her elbow, although he lingered in helping her arm back into the sleeve and kissed the smooth delicate curve of her honey-gold shoulder. Vinney drew back sharply at the touch of his lips on her skin and in the short embarrassed silence that followed she felt suddenly repentant and naïve.

"I'm sorry. You've been very kind. I hope you'll always be my friend." Her smile was warm and sincere, and she offered him her hand. "Goodbye. I can walk back to the village to collect Prince."

Nick took her hand surveying her face with an ironic stare. "Prince is here – I sent for him. Be careful how you go."

He dropped her hand and the temperature of the room seemed to drop with it. Then they were outside and walking around the front of the house to a wrought iron door set in the stone wall at the side. He let her through into a stone-flagged courtyard filled on two sides with horse boxes and he strode across to one. Vinney watched while he led Prince out, the man and the horse both magnificent specimens of male virility. Then she moved forward to put up her hand gently to Prince and smile fondly into the long-lashed big eyes. The next moment she was in the saddle with Prince's powerful muscles firm and solid as a rock beneath her.

Nick was looking up at her with an expression she could not read – searching, quizzical – she couldn't tell. That mobile mouth of his which she knew could readily curve into a smile was set ironically. She had a wild urge to fling herself down into his arms and seek comfort from burrowing into his wide shoulder. But she had been on the receiving end of so many rebuffs that caution died hard.

In a small voice she said, "Goodbye, Nick. Thanks again."

60

"Goodbye," coolly.

Vinney rode out of the courtyard seeing his hand lifted in a salute in a mist of tears. If anyone had told her years ago that she would fall in love with the kind of man her sister Denise had chosen, she would have laughed at the absurdity of it. But it was true – she had fallen in love with her sister's fiancé. What now? If she had any sense she would run and go on running from situations which could only end in bringing her more heartache.

The ride back to Brown Thatch was short and exhilarating, but it did nothing to clear her brain of confused thoughts. Once in the sanctuary of her room she steeled herself to face hard facts, bracing herself to review her problems candidly without apprehension. She would not falter even though her heart was so involved. What did she see? A girl held down by the iron chains of a tragic past whose return home was made in order to break those chains. But how? One way would be to insist upon her mother knowing the truth about what really had happened. Then it was only Denise's word against her own. Furthermore, her accident and the fact of Nick taking her back to his place would be all over the village by now – how long would it take to reach Brown Thatch via her mother's friends? When it did Denise would swear that her sister had made the whole story up in order to turn Nick away from her so that she could have him for herself.

Head and heart aching, Vinney walked to look up at her father's photograph on the wall of her room. What would he have done in similar circumstances? She gazed hopelessly at the serene countenance, every feature enriched by a strength of character. He would never have run away with a jaw like that. With a deep heartfelt sigh, Vinney retreated a little. Pale as a lily, she made her decision to stay.

The next morning Sandy awakened her with a cup of tea. "Denise wants to see you in her room," she said. "Something to do with a carrier bag of things you bought from the village yesterday. You left them at Mr. Wentworth's place and he sent them over this morning."

Sandy, poker-faced, vouchsafed this information and left the room, leaving Vinney fully prepared with the knowledge that already Denise and probably her mother had been informed of the incident involving Nick Wentworth's car. She drank her tea, and any foreboding of trouble was lessened by the fact that Sandy was a little on her side, otherwise she would not have warned her what to expect.

Denise's bedroom was vastly different from her own. It was bigger, had a much nicer view and had been decorated in pale turquoise and silver panels. The carpet was a lush off-white like the built-in bedroom furniture. The dressing table mirrors reflected on crystal bottles of expensive perfume, and Vinney looked swiftly away from a photograph of Nick, head and shoulders, on the bedside table.

"Come in. Don't stand there like an owl," Denise said rudely. The brown eyes snapped with malice and a hint of amusement. "A good likeness, don't you agree?"

Vinney stared at her stupidly and watched her set down her cup and saucer. She was sitting up in bed. The delicately strapped bodice of the Empire-top nightdress revealed the roundness of her bust and a thick rope of dark brown hair over one shoulder made her brown eyes even darker.

"I beg your pardon," Vinney said coldly. "I don't know what you're talking about."

"Oh, come off it." A red-tipped hand reached for a packet of cigarettes from the bedside table and well manicured fingers zipped on a lighter. The dark brown eyes watching the trail of smoke shooting from her lips ceilingward were bright with amusement. "I'm afraid you can't do anything here without it spreading around like a bush fire. I mean Nick and you throwing yourself into his arms in full view of the shoppers in the village yesterday."

Vinney kept her temper with an effort. The village grapevine had evidently lost no time in getting to work. Her lip curled. "I was almost knocked down by his car," she vouchsafed evenly. "I stepped right into the path of it and was lucky that he happened to be a good driver. I might have been killed."

Denise threw back her head and looked insolently down

her nose at her.

"So you nearly got yourself killed and you threw yourself into his arms instead in gratitude?"

Vinney simmered. It was bad enough to be treated like a leper in her own home, but to be treated so insolently by her own sister was something not to be tolerated, especially since she herself was taking the blame for something Denise had done ten years ago.

Righteous anger darkened her blue eyes. But she kept a steady look, as her hands clasped the back of a chair. She said coolly and clearly, "What I do is no concern of yours. You talk over what you've heard with Nick Wentworth, not with me. And don't you dare summon me to your room again like a servant – not that I rate myself better than a servant. In fact I couldn't imagine anyone as low as you."

Denise laughed and held her cigarette negligently between her fingers.

"My dear Vinney, losing your temper will get you nowhere. I think you ought to hear what I've got to say."

The silken tones halted Vinney on her way to the door and she turned round slowly. "Make it brief. I feel stifled in the same room with you," she said coldly.

"It's about our Nick," Denise began, and smiled in triumph at her sister's reaction. "Ah, I thought that would interest you! You've gone as stiff as a rod. He makes love very nicely, doesn't he?"

Vinney paled with anger. "That's a leading question, of course. I wouldn't know."

Denise became interested in the dull glowing end of her cigarette.

"You wouldn't know either that he's come into a fortune besides the house. Colonel Davenport Wentworth left a fortune and the house to Nick."

Vinney's chin lifted. "I don't believe it! Nick said he had been left the house . . . and . . ."

"He didn't mention the money," Denise cut in. "He would have been a fool not to, wouldn't he? That would have made him the most eligible man for miles around, wouldn't it?"

"I'd say he was the most eligible man around without his money."

"So would I. But then I'm prejudiced in his favour, since I have his ring."

The words filled the quiet room and Denise laughed as she left her bed and reached for a wrap on a nearby chair after stubbing out her cigarette. Vinney watched as she tied the silken cord around her waist and noticed the deep brown nicotine stain on her fingers. It occurred to her then that there was a reason for her heavy smoking. There was something on her mind and it had nothing to do with what happened ten years ago. She had shrugged that off years ago. No, it had to be something else.

She spoke almost without volition. "I don't believe you are engaged to Nick Wentworth," she stated baldly.

"No? Then what's this?" A white arm shot up and the emerald scintillated on her hand. "I assure you he did give this to me and that it's quite valuable."

"Like your clothes," Vinney took her up sharply. "Where do you get the money from for everything? I know Daddy left Mummy comfortably off, but not to that extent, and you don't work."

"Ah, but I do – or rather I did. I was a model until I had a silly accident and hurt my kneecap. Now I can't stand for long intervals and I'm recuperating hoping my knee will eventually be as good as new."

"In the meantime you're hoping to marry Nick Wentworth and then all your troubles will be over?" Vinney's lip curled again. "You would marry him for his money."

Denise moved to the dressing table and picked up a hairbrush to draw it slowly and thoughtfully down the silken rope of hair.

"He would have been glad to have me anyway. He's like me in a way – he knows what he wants and sets out to get it. And he'd hold anything he won against all comers. We both have a primitive streak in us, but he happens to be stubborn too." The brown eyes meeting Vinney's were brittle and cold. "I met him abroad while on a modelling job in Sri Lanka.

He fell for me all right and we became engaged. He had six months' leave coming to him and he was going to spend it with his uncle, Colonel Davenport Wentworth. He was going to take me back as his wife."

Vinney recoiled as from a blow below the belt. Common sense told her her sister was lying, but the emerald winked maliciously as Denise brushed her hair, and focussed on her Vinney's engrossed face.

"In the meantime," she continued, "the Colonel died and Nick came on a short visit to the funeral. He came unexpectedly and found me with Peter Trevira. We were making love in his car. We had a terrible row and the engagement was off, but Nick didn't ask for the ring. Mummy doesn't know, neither does Grandmother. They still think it's on. So now you know why I shall never admit that it was my fault Daddy died. At the moment I have a chance with Nick, but if he discovered my secret everything would be over."

Vinney gasped with surprise. "But why are you telling me this? I could easily tell him the truth about you."

"But you won't, will you? Denise put down the brush and turned to face her. "For the simple reason that I would deny it with everything I had, and you'd hardly marry him with that stigma hanging over your head, would you?"

White to the lips, Vinney turned and opened the door, to hear Denise fire a parting shot.

"'What a nice bedtime story for Aunty Denise to tell to your children! Once upon a time there was a very naughty little girl who disobeyed her mother and went into the sea . . .'"

The door clicked shut and Vinney went slowly to her room.

CHAPTER FOUR

VINNEY had breakfasted alone, and washed the used dishes along with others on the draining board in the kitchen before going to her room. The next half hour or so was taken up with chores such as straightening and dusting her room. She was collecting her writing materials when her mother called from the corridor and approached her open door.

"If you're going out," she said on the threshold, "you might take Gran her pills."

She looked very smart in pale blue slacks, tailored white blouse and a beige suede jerkin. Her slender expressive hands, that would have stood her in good stead as an actress, were fingering a small packet. Her brown eyes were neither friendly nor unfriendly as they rested upon her fair beauty. Her reluctant appraisal was the limit of her greeting.

Beneath her scrutiny, Vinney moistened dry lips. That self-control was another admirable trait for acting, she thought, she really is beautiful, I wish I knew what she really thinks of me, by what twist of emotion she can love one child so much and the other not at all. The tang of seaweed and flowers drifted across the room from the open window, perfumed yet bittersweet.

Try to be friendly. Be impersonal and pleasant – yes, that was it. Keeping these meetings with her mother on an un-emotional level would simplify matters a great deal. Her own vague uneasiness must never again end in actual discomfort. After all, this was her mother. The word seemed to taunt her. Something stabbed at Vinney's heart, as her mother continued.

"The chemist gave them to me yesterday. While I know she is not without any I would like her to have them as soon as possible. By the way, I hope you and Denise are hitting it off," she added. "I want Denise to settle down in a home of her own more than anything. She needs a man's firm hand. Nick Wentworth is an ideal match, wealthy and masterful

enough to curb her wild spirits. I have to mention this because there has been talk," she finished.

Vinney's colour rose, then receded, leaving her face ashen. forced from a raw throat.

"There's always talk in a village, meaningless talk." Her chin lifted. "I'll take the pills. Thanks." She took the small packet thoughtfully. "Is Gran ill?"

"No. But it's essential for her to take the pills regularly. I don't know if you know about her." Grace Brandon paused.

Ice crept up to Vinney's heart. "Know what?" she said.

"That Gran had a slight heart attack ten years ago just after you left for Malta. Delayed shock, the doctor said. After all, Daddy was her only son."

There was nothing unkind or malicious in her tones. She was merely stating a fact, and Vinney felt the past washing over her in deep depressing waves. "I'm sorry. If I could wipe out the past, I would. I wasn't entirely to blame," she said through pale lips, but her mother was already moving along the corridor towards the staircase. Vinney hesitated, then walked back slowly into her room, picked up her shoulder bag, and dropping the pills inside, went downstairs.

She had intended to spend the morning writing letters to her friends in Malta. The early spring air was not warm enough to go down to the beach to write them and perhaps take a book to while away the hours. However, the delivery of her grandmother's pills took precedence over her plans and she resolved to walk across the fields forming part of a short cut between Brown Thatch and the old lady's charming villa. The garden in front of the house was already bright with spring flowers and a white Persian cat lay curled up between two earthenware pots of geraniums fast asleep at the front door. He raised his head and two topaz eyes surveyed her sleepily before he rolled over on his back purring at her approach.

Vinney laughed softly and bent down to tickle him as two feet in very serviceable shoes appeared nearby. Looking up to the figure attached to them, she saw the smiling rather plain face of Miss Tatten the housekeeper.

Vinney said awkwardly, "Good morning, Miss Tatten.

I've called with the pills Mummy collected from the village for my grandmother. I hope she's well." She straightened and took the pills from her bag as she spoke.

"Perfectly well," was the quiet answer still accompanied by a warm smile. "Do come in and give them to her yourself, Miss Vinney."

Vinney shook her head. "I'd rather not, if you don't mind. Give her my love."

Poor Grandmother, she thought, retracing her footsteps back to Brown Thatch. Like Mummy, she's an unhappy woman, lonely and embittered by those tragic blows in life that many women find too much to cope with. Grandfather Brandon had lost his life at sea and had gone down with his ship fighting for his country. Then her father had gone and now Aunt Phyllis had gone too.

Vinney sighed in deep compassion. She was genuinely anxious to become friends with her grandmother, for it was up to her, as her father's daughter, to atone – as much as love and friendship could atone – for what had happened years ago. If only it was possible to break through that barrier of reserve her grandmother lived behind? Only by doing so could she hope for any response to her own overtures in that direction. Later, if they ever became close, her grandmother might feel more kindly disposed towards her and not judge her too harshly. It was a comforting thought.

Lunch was over, and Vinney, having heard her sister drive away from the house en route for the doctor's for treatment to her injured knee, felt a feeling of loneliness wash over her. Her mother had gone out also on one of her many commitments to do with charities and social engagements and had not asked her to accompany her. She could go to the riding school to help out if she felt inclined. But for the present Vinney was in no way ready to mix with the community as yet. People were so curious, blatantly so, and she was hypersensitive at the moment to what kind of reception she would receive. In the end she spent the afternoon on Prince, cantering along the deserted shore at speed with his hooves thudding rhythmically on the firm sand before taking one of the bridle paths ranging within a few miles of Brown Thatch.

Vinney lingered to take a last reassuring look at herself in the mirror before leaving with her mother and sister for the Hunt Ball. Her reflection was pleasing. The dress, simple in design, had layer upon layer of a filmy diaphanous midnight blue nipped in at her slender waist beneath a swathed bodice. The diamond necklace glittered at her throat along with the matching ear-rings and her hair, freshly shampooed and dressed by Antonio that afternoon, completed a vision of loveliness at which she now stared unbelievingly. Is it really me? she thought wistfully. Antonio is a wizard.

In the hall, her mother eyed her critically. Midnight blue, the colour for blondes, enhanced the dark violet softness of her eyes, her delicately modelled face beneath the beautifully dressed golden hair showed strength of character besides prettiness, thought Grace Brandon. The girl was lovely with a poignant loveliness which, although she would not admit it, caught at her heart strings. Then Vinney was forgotten as Grace elegant in an evening dress of silver grey chiffon with a v-neck and cape bodice enhanced by a triple row of pearls around her throat, turned to greet Denise.

Denise was looking stunningly attractive in a figure-hugging dress of silver lamé with a deceptively swirling full skirt. Her thick, lustrous hair hung provocatively forward over her shoulder and her slumbrous eyes in their frame of lashes looked at Vinney with a strange implacability.

They were among the first arrivals and in the room where they shed their wraps Vinney was delighted to see Susan from the riding school. Contrary to her expectations, Vinney was soon surrounded with partners. Everyone seemed to know who she was, and she threw herself into the enjoyment of the evening light of heart and feet.

The ballroom with its crystal chandeliers and elegant chairs placed back against panelled walls was ideal for dancing. In the arms of her partner, Vinney saw Denise dancing with Nick who had brought them in his car and her mother dancing with Charles Trevira. Peter was following Denise around the room with narrowed eyes and appeared oblivious of willing partners who hovered near. Vinney felt sorry for him and longed to tell him that strong man tactics were the only kind Denise understood – like Nick Wentworth's, for example. Denise had admitted that they were two of a kind. They certainly made a handsome couple. Then, because it made her miserable to see them together, Vinney very determinedly dismissed them from her mind.

She danced the last number before the interval with Susan's husband, Tim, and, on the last beat, they went in search of Susan. Vinney was following Tim through the crowd of dancers when someone caught her arm.

Nick Wentworth was looking down at her with a half mocking expression of tender amusement.

"At last," he murmured. "I've been longing with bared teeth and much gnashing of gums to tear you away from an endless string of partners – or shall I say admirers?"

"What about you?" Vinney felt strangely lighthearted. "I bet you never gave me a thought while you were dancing with all the pretty girls until you just bumped into me."

Careful now, her heart warmed as her dancing eyes took in the arrogant features so far above her own. Tall, dark and handsome with a dangerous charm to boot, four reasons why she should keep her distance even if he were free, which he was not entirely.

"Shame on you and may you be forgiven," he whispered, a firm hand on her arm. "Here was I, hungry as a hunter, yet willing to forgo my supper if need be in my search for you. Come on to battle stations"

The buffet was laid in the dining room on an enormously long table agleam with glass and silver and almost groaning with the weight of food. Nick settled her in a corner at a small table behind an enormous shrub in an outsize pot and joined the throng of people surrounding the table amid the popping of champagne corks and much laughter and chatter.

When he returned with a tray bearing drinks and two generously laden plates filled with an assortment of mouth-watering delicacies, he put them on the table and drew up a chair very close to her own.

"Now come on, tuck in, there's a good girl. There's plenty more where this came from." His dark eyes were intent upon her startled look, and he grinned.

She said on a gasp, "But I can't eat half this!"

"That's right. Not half. All of it, and there's champagne to wash it down. Afterwards you can dance it off with me."

Vinney did not know whether it was the champagne or the nearness of Nick's ironic gaze that seemed to make her a little lightheaded. But all the feed went, the wafer-thin sandwiches filled with every conceivable kind of meat, the feather-light little pastries overflowing with savoury concoctions, the delicious little fruits frosted with sugar and the fingers of pastry filled with cream cheese and topped with nuts were all washed down with the champagne.

When they had finished he rose indolently to his feet and gave her his slow disturbing smile, and her heart tilted. "More?" he asked.

"My goodness! No, thanks. I've had an adequate sufficiency. I'm sure I won't be able to dance a step after stuffing myself regardless." She had to laugh then, feeling the bubbles from the champagne in her eyes. "You're a bad influence on me. Do you know that?"

Nick stood for several moments holding the tray of used dishes and looking down at her with his usual searching, quizzical expression.

"There's nothing wrong in getting someone into the party mood to . . . er . . . to dance." The pause was deliberate with his eyes filled with devilment. "A moment ago you had stars in those marvellous dark blue eyes. Now they look a little scared. Don't run away – stay where you are. I'll be back."

He came back with a minute to spare for them to stroll back to the ballroom where she entered into the warm circle of his arms and closed her eyes. They had circled the room when she opened them again to see Denise. She was sitting with a group of young people watching the dancers and idly tapping the ash from her cigarette into an ash tray on the small, low table by her elbow. She was on the fringe of the party, and Vinney had the feeling she was looking for her. When their eyes met she stiffened slightly and Nick looked down into her face. "What's the matter? You've gone as stiff as a rod," he demanded.

"Nothing is the matter. Perhaps I'm tired."

"You're not tired, you're scared – scared of your own sister. Why?"

"You're far too discerning," she complained.

"True. I am where you're concerned."

Vinney looked up at him warily. "Why? You hardly know me. And stop feeling sorry for me!"

His smile was steely. "I'm not feeling sorry for you, I'm feeling sorry for myself. Do you want to know why?"

Her eyes followed the attractive tilt of his eyebrows and her heart missed a beat. "You're unhappy because you're still in love with Denise and you're too proud to admit it," she suggested evenly.

"Am I?" laconically.

"Of course you are, otherwise why did you not ask for your ring back?"

He swung her round out of the path of a couple. His hand was on her back and Vinney had the feeling that it was touching her heart.

"Did Denise tell you that?" he demanded.

Ever truthful, she said, "Denise told me why you broke off the engagement. I think she still loves you, if that's any comfort to you."

"It isn't – and now let's forget Denise, shall we?"

He drew her closer and they drifted smoothly around the room. Denise was indeed forgotten, the music was low and sweet, the lights dimmed and Vinney had wings on her feet. It was the nearest she had ever been to heaven and she had neither the will nor the desire to resist.

Vinney, mounted on Prince, rode leisurely along the bridle path leading through the woods verging on Nick Wentworth's estate. Overhead arched a ceiling of virgin blue sky etched by the young spring green of swaying trees. Each day she was finding an increasing pleasure in Prince's company. She appreciated him as only a girl who counted for so little in the lives of her family could do. During the week she had been at home, Vinney was learning to regard herself as being outside their lives. Neither her mother nor Denise had bothered to accept her and there had been no word from her grandmother inviting her over for tea. Useless to tell herself that she didn't care, because the thought of it cast a shadow over the beauty around her, blurring the green of the trees and the blue sky until even the sweet little chirrups of the birds passed by unheeded.

The path she had taken was only one of many leading through woods which could be on the Wentworth estate. Years ago there had been gamekeepers and the tall angry figure of Colonel Davenport Wentworth to warn that the grounds were private. But that was a long while ago in the days of her youth. However, the fact that she could be trespassing did not trouble her overmuch since a delightful little spinney now came into view and a gnarled old stump of a tree was just asking for her to loop Prince's reins around it. The mellow spring warmth of the sun did the rest and she dismounted, tied up Prince, leaving him free to roam a little, and settled herself down in a small grassy hollow.

The soft rustling silence around her was very soothing, but now it was the thought of Nick Wentworth that tormented. She had not seen him since the night of the Hunt Ball, but the recollection of that night still sent her pulses racing a little. In spite of herself something feminine in her had answered to the fiercely arrogant maleness in him. Emotions lying dormant in her had been rudely aroused as she had danced in his arms until she had been conscious only of a half exultant, half frightened thrill of surrendering. Now, with the thoughts of it accelerating her pulses again, Vinney felt angry for ever having given in to his charm. It had been most unfair to Denise, who was still in love with him. Moreover, if she was falling in love with him herself – already had – at least she could keep the fact a secret and make sure it went no further than a crush on a very charming, very persistent young man. There was such a thing as playing the game even with a sister who obviously had no time for her – which was no reason for her not to be straight herself. What if she were to be weak and seek the solace of Nick's arms away from them all? How could she bear to face the ultimate result – that of taking away her sister's fiancé on the top of what had happened ten years ago? Besides, he could be looking for an affair to ease his boredom ...

Her thoughts snapped off with the sharpness of a breaking twig. For an instant she was stupefied and doubting the evidence of her own eyes. Then her faculties grouped themselves together and she blinked. He was sitting on the other side of the hollow, lolling back against the stalwart trunk of an old tree with a kind of indolent grace. The sun shone on his well polished riding boots and frolicked in the crisp tobacco brown hair, giving his face a lean, tanned strength of its own. He was looking at her in a contemplative way as though he was studying her.

Her heart leapt sickeningly. But her voice, under control and deadly even, said, "How long have you been here? Is this a joke?"

He laughed, his teeth a bar of whiteness in his tanned face. "You mean have I been following you? No, I haven't. I happen to be on home ground. This is part of the estate." His eyes were mocking. "And I was here first. Been here some time doubting the evidence of my own eyes."

"That makes two of us," Vinney answered coldly. "And now, if you'll excuse me ..."

She moved, but before she could spring up to her feet he was beside her, looking down into her large troubled eyes.

"Vinney! What is this?" That deep note in his voice when he spoke her name twisted her heart. What a weak spineless creature she was, to be so influenced by his charming technique. She didn't speak. He was all laughter and charm, as he spoke again. "Aren't you happy to see me?"

Vinney took a long breath that came from deep inside her. "I'm always happy to see a . . . friend. And now I must go," she mumbled, and rose to her feet.

His face set and he spoke with an impersonal deliberation.

74

"Is that all you have to say to me?" He had gripped her shoulders as he spoke, tense and unsmiling. "What kind of a girl are you? What is it you're afraid of . . . love . . . your own shadow?"

His savage tone hurt more than the painful grip of his hands, but she kept her eyes on his controlled, dark, expressionless face.

Defensively, she began, "I came home to be reconciled with my family. You know the reason I went away, so you'll understand why I came back. I promised myself I wouldn't become involved with anyone until I'd settled my own conscience. I don't want nightmares for the rest of my life – especially an added one of having stolen my sister's fiancé."

"I am not your sister's fiancé," he said tightly, and hauled her into his arms. "You little idiot! Don't you know that I love you – have done from the first moment I saw you?"

He kissed her, a hard, possessive kiss which lifted her to dizzy heights. Inwardly, Vinney groaned. The urge to tell him the truth about ten years ago, that ever-pressing and insistent need to tell him, burned inside her like a fever. Then common sense prevailed. He was engaged to Denise. He could be taking her, Vinney, on the rebound. Just because she was on the same wavelength with him it did not mean that he was on the same wavelength with herself. He knew now that she loved him – how could he not when her lips responded and her bones seemed to melt beneath the fire of his passion? He would think it was because of Denise that she was holding back. But it was much more than that. Much, much more.

"Please," she begged when at last she could speak, "Don't make me do something that I could regret all my life."

His arms dropped and his face was an expressionless mask. "Thanks," he said. "At least we know where we stand."

She stared up at him pitifully and was silent. A few minutes later she bade him goodbye formally from the back of Prince before riding away.

It had been a busy morning for Vinney, an early ride on Prince before breakfast, her room to clean and then a session in the kitchen garden picking vegetables for Sandy and flowers for her room. Her mother looked after the flowers for the house, arranging them beautifully to her own satisfaction, so Vinney did not intrude. It was a lonely existence with only Sandy to talk to. "Sandy," she said warily as she peeled potatoes quite voluntarily, "you've known Mummy longer than I have. Why doesn't she like me . . . I mean, she never has."

Sandy was seasoning a pot roast and went on with her task in silence. Her mouth tightened primly. "It's not my place to tell you anything about your family – and you shouldn't be in my kitchen getting under my feet."

"I know," Vinney admitted, unperturbed by the disapproving growl. "I just thought that you might help me settle my mind on certain things that have puzzled me through the years."

Sandy was stubborn and did not reply, so Vinney said no more. Finishing the potatoes, she washed her hands, made coffee for herself and tea for her companion because she preferred it.

"There you are," she said, gently pushing Sandy into her favourite chair. "Where did you put those Vienna biscuits I brought for you? You see, I hadn't forgotten that you liked them."

Sandy waved a gnarled hand in the direction of the Welsh dresser as she accepted the cup of tea. Then she glowered at the chocolate Vienna biscuits being presented to her on a plate.

"No use bribing me, my girl," she said darkly.

But Vinney only laughed. "I had no idea of bribing you, my sweet," she vouchsafed. "You nearly didn't get them. They went for a Burton with all the other things I bought that day when I took a dive into the gutter. Fortunately, they didn't get wet."

"So I heard. You know Nick Wentworth is engaged to your sister, don't you?"

Vinney drank part of her coffee. If Sandy was going to be close so was she. "Denise showed me her ring on the day I arrived," she admitted. "I've no intention of taking him away from her."

"Glad to hear it." Sandy bit into a biscuit and looked more friendly. "One thing I've always liked about you is that you've no malicious streak in you, never have had. Not like somebody I could name, Anyway, I don't suppose it will do any harm if I tell you a little about your mother. She never wanted a second baby. When you came she resented you bitterly."

"But why?" Vinney asked.

Sandy shrugged and finished her biscuit. "Well, your father was away for long periods at sea and she hated staying in the house when he was away. She was a repertory actress when she married and saw your father's work in the Navy as an excellent opportunity for her to continue with her career. When Denise was two she took her touring with her in a small company and she gradually climbed the ladder to bigger parts on the stage. Then came the opportunity of a lifetime, a leading role she'd been waiting for, with top billing in the West End, and when your father came home on leave they celebrated the occasion. When he went back to his ship, he left her pregnant. She never forgave him for robbing her of the opportunity which only comes to some people once in a lifetime, and she bitterly resented you."

Vinney stared in front of her bleakly. "Poor Mummy! She would be filled with remorse when Daddy died just as I was."

"Your grandmother doesn't like her," added Sandy. "Never has."

Vinney smiled sadly. "Most mothers resent the woman who takes their place in their son's life."

The music of Beethoven's Third Symphony filtered softly into the room. Vinney lay back in her chair, letting the peace of it flow over her. In the oppressing atmosphere of Brown Thatch her spirit was wilting. From the hot sun and the warmth of friends in Malta she had come home to find the coolness of the air intensified by the coldness of indifference. The trouble was she had nothing in common with the community around her except for her love of riding. Susan and

Tim were her very good friends, but they were a married couple and were engrossed in each other. Her mother and sister had carved out their own particular niche in life which did not include herself. She was the cuckoo in the nest. They simply were not interested, which left her – where? In a limbo, between days of wretched soul-searching, until she claimed the refuge of her bed.

The days were passing slowly, each one rife with the thought that she should not have left Malta, at any rate not so completely as to sever all contact. Yet what could she do? Demand a confrontation with Denise in front of her mother – stick it out courageously with a smile in the belief that truth will out eventually – pack her cases and leave or search for subtle weapons with which to persuade Denise to come clean, as it were?

She had an opportunity of following the first course open to her, the one of confrontation at dinner that evening when she dined with her mother and sister alone. But her lips simply could not form the words. It would only end in her being humiliated, encompassed by bitter words and subterfuge. So she sat silent with the feeling that each mouthful of food would choke her. After dinner she went to her room. She did not sleep, of course, but lay there in her costly silk pyjamas seeking some way to go on that was more bearable. She was fighting in her corner and had received no quarter, nor was likely to. Then the only answer was to fight back. This she could do, first by being determinedly cheerful, then she would storm the fort, gracefully, refusing to be locked out. Once within the gates, as it were, she would be more able to feel her way to some compromise on the part of Denise. Then, and only then, could she go away free from the stigma of having been the cause of her father's death.

CHAPTER FIVE

VINNEY sat at the piano playing a delightful piece of Chopin. Shadows deepened in the graciously furnished room until the proud, immaculate head resting back against a cushion stood out starkly white. Firelight flickered on Grandmother Brandon's closed eyes as she relaxed in her roomy, comfortable chair with her feet on a tapestry-covered footstool.

Vinney had been asked to come to tea that afternoon after sending her grandmother a bouquet of flowers. Miss June at the post office had told her that her grandmother had not been well and was suffering from a cold, so she had sent the spray of flowers with a little get well card, hence the invitation. She had gone, delighted to think that her grandmother could be thawing a little towards her, and it was with satisfaction and a lifting of her spirits that she had set off on the short journey from Brown Thatch.

Miss Tatten, the housekeeper, had met her at the door, smiling with her usual warmth, and had shown her into the lounge where she was welcomed with surprising cordiality by her grandmother.

"Come in child," she said. "How nice of you to send me the flowers and to accept my invitation to tea when I'd been so unpleasant to you. I had no right to sit in judgement just because – of what happened years ago. It was silly of me to act the way I did after you'd brought me that shawl from Phyllis." She turned and sat down, leaving Vinney to take a chair nearby. She went on frankly, "I've been doing a lot of thinking, and I'm afraid I've become an embittered old woman. To begin with I lost my husband, my daughter married and went to live in Mai a, then my son, your father, married a woman who chose to travel the country on the stage, taking my granddaughter with her. When you were born your mother, of course, came hon e, but things were not the same

. . . and then . . . I was very bitter when my son was taken from me."

Vinney was suddenly very pale with the memory of the tragedy of so long ago. A chill feathered over her skin but her blue eyes smiled understandingly. "Yes, I know. I wanted to die myself at the time and I suppose you did too. Believe me, if I could have given my life for Daddy's I would have done gladly."

She was not finding the part she was playing any too easy. It did not help to know that, when she was planning to be friendly towards her grandmother, the old lady was genuinely sorry and anxious to be friends. Unhappiness darkened her eyes and her pathetically curved lips.

"You always were a nice child. I hope we're going to be friends." The older woman's eyes, as deeply blue as her granddaughter's rested affectionately on the flower-like face.

"I'm sure we are." Vinney blinked back the tears. "And I've so much to tell you about Aunt Phyllis and our life in Malta." A smile broke through and she added quickly, "I've heaps of photographs, reels of film that I can show on a screen for you to see."

Her grandmother smiled back. "You have? You must come and show them to me. Thank you, my dear."

During tea, encouraged by the older woman's eager, interested questions, Vinney talked happily about life in Malta and included several amusing incidents which soon had her grandmother rocking in her chair. When she left the old lady was fast asleep in her chair with a look of happiness on her face which heartened Vinney, knowing she had helped to put it there.

There was a slight breeze to greet her on her homeward journey and the air seemed to crackle with freshness from the sea. The sky was filled with stars and the tide was well out when she walked slowly along the beach with a spring in her step that had not been there on her outward journey. She was friends with her grandmother, and something proud and radiant came into her face. Her chin lifted.

"Good evening," said Nick Wentworth, looming suddenly

from the shadows. "Do you usually take walks alone at night?"

Vinney gave a startled gasp. "Do you usually creep upon people to give them a shock?" she retorted breathlessly.

Her heart had somersaulted and she trembled as he took her arm. It was enough, more than enough. His touch, the fraught intimacy, the utter obliviousness of everything around her, said it all. Vinney hoped he would not sense her confusion as he steered her through the purple shadows. Her nerve ends tingled in her finger tips. A swift look sideways told her he was more disturbing and handsome than ever before, his body supple, his lazy nonchalance tearing at her heart.

His mouth was near to her ear. "I creep up on all my women and ravish them. So beware," he whispered, and shook with inward mirth. "Miss me?"

She rallied very well, remembering the game she was playing and the resolve to remain sparklingly alert.

"Should I? Have you been away?"

"Touché!" His exaggerated wince dispelled his mirth. "I don't know whether to beat you or kiss you until you beg my pardon. Of course I've been away. I had to go to London for a discussion with the executors of my uncle's will. It was made years ago and the small legacy he made to the people who worked for him is a mere pittance today."

"So you increased it. That was noble of you. You're a nice man, Nick." Vinney bit her lip. Far too nice for Denise, she thought.

"I could be nicer if you'd give me the chance," he smiled.

The perfume of the night isolated them from a world where time was standing still, as still as her heart. Oh no, this can't be. I don't want this to happen – not now anyway. I want to clear myself of the shadow hanging over my head like the sword of Damocles, Vinney moaned inwardly. I'm afraid of what the past can do to me.

Aloud, she said, "Off with the old love and on with the new. Is that it, Nick?"

His eyes searched her face in the dusk. He gripped her shoulders, grim and unsmiling. "You little fool! Can't you see the real thing when it happens between two people like you and me? I love you. Don't you understand?"

"I don't want to understand," she mumbled. "You've heard of the way my father died, that . . . that I – through my wilfulness – killed him. If you think anything of me at all, leave me alone – just leave me alone!"

He walked her home and all his arguments were put against a blank wall. At the gates of Brown Thatch Vinney looked up at him. "I'm sorry, Nick. There's something I have to do, something that I can't tell anyone about, not even you. Until I've done what I know I must do, there's no place for anyone in my life."

He stared down into her face, his hand on her shoulders, then they slid down her arms and he hauled her against him. His lips fastened on hers and her mouth was soft and sweet. She clung and trembled. When he let her go his deep voice smote her heart.

"It's no use fighting, my sweet. You and I belong together. You're mine and I can take you any time I want to – don't forget that."

Dazedly, Vinney watched him take his leave without a backward glance. Seeing him again had awakened every need of him which, she thought, had been crushed out during his absence. With every beat of her heart, she wanted him, and as that crying need slowly left her, she came back to remembering her resolve. She had decided to fight for her own self-respect and the fact that it was proving a harder fight than she had anticipated made no difference. With the same youthful courage with which she had overcome her father's death, a courage which had kept her proudly silent when her family had cast her out, she now faced this new, shattering decision.

Prince gave a delighted whinney as Vinney rode him into the stable yard at the riding school. She had come in answer to a telephone call from Susan received while she was having breakfast that morning.

"Do come as soon as you can. I've some marvellous news and if I don't keep talking about it I'll burst!" Susan's voice brought an air of light-heartedness to the quiet house and Vinney found herself smiling as she went to saddle Prince.

What a difference a home made with love in it, she thought wistfully, and wondered what it was that Susan was burning to tell her.

Susan was alone in the big, warm kitchen and the kettle was on the boil.

"Come in, Vinney. Mrs. Shane is out and Tim is in the surgery."

Slim brown hands were busily making tea and cheeks of bright colour emphasised the shining dark eyes. Susan looked like a cheeky little red robin with her long, slim legs in black slacks and the scarlet sweater on her short body.

"No cake for me, please," Vinney laughingly objected. "I've only just had breakfast."

"It's parkin. It'll do you good. I'm having a piece and you can't let me eat alone." Susan cut a second generous piece of the parkin and put it on a plate for herself. "And now for my news." She drew a deep breath. "I bet you can't wait."

Vinney laughed as they both sat down at the table. "I'm waiting."

Susan looked longingly at the parkin and decided to say her piece first. "I'm going to have a baby," she said, and her colour deepened.

Vinney was radiant. "No wonder you look beautiful! I'm delighted. Does Tim know?"

Susan nodded on a mouthful of parkin and swallowed it. "He's way up in the clouds this morning. He says he'll be a bit worried because it's my first one," she gurgled. "My first one, mind you – I don't know how many he's thinking of having!"

"But you want children, don't you, Susan?" Vinney's smile was very sweet, very wistful.

"Oh yes. Only . . . well, there doesn't seem to be many prospects for children today, with all the violence and everything." Susan dealt with another bite of parkin and sighed. "I've just thought of something else too. I shall grow fat and ungainly. I hope Tim doesn't go off me." Her brown eyes moved slowly over Vinney's heavy cream jersey, the elegant suede jerkin culminating into well cut riding breeches and long soft leather boots with a handmade air. "I wish I was elegant and sophisticated like you. You'll look beautiful even when you're expecting a baby. Tim admires you enormously."

Vinney looked startled. "Does he? How nice of him. But he loves you, Susan, never forget that. He did the proposing, you didn't. And no more torturing yourself with silly notions. Don't you know that since your marriage you've become beautiful, and the beauty all has something to do with something inside you, an inner glow because you know you're loved. And that, after all, is what every woman wants in the end, above all material things."

Susan stared at her blankly and the words took some time to register. Then the hands that had shaken a little and spilled her tea grew suddenly steady in mid-air. Slim, brown fingers curled more confidently around the cup. Her smile was brilliant.

"Yes, I see what you mean," she breathed happily. "I'm an idiot to let all these doubts crowd in on my happiness." Her brown eyes widened as a thought struck her. "You know, we spend most of our lives worrying about things that never happen and things that simply don't matter."

Vinney nodded. "I like the parkin. Tell Mrs. Shane she hasn't lost the magic in her fingers."

Susan nodded and they munched together in silence. "More tea?" She leaned over to replenish her guest's cup and said curiously, "I've often thought about you and Denise – the two prettiest girls in the village and yet both of you are still single. I saw Denise yesterday with Nick Wentworth." She paused and replenished her own cup, then put down the tea-pot. "I hope you don't mind me saying this, but I've never been much for your sister and I think Nick is much too nice for her. He'd suit you."

It was Vinney's turn to hold her cup with trembling hands and spill her tea until she lowered the cup carefully into the saucer. Her laugh was one that did not ring true in her own ears.

"Now don't tell me you're turning into a match-maker,"

she said lightly. "It's a dangerous game. Perhaps it's as well that you're going to be busy with your little brood."

"That's just it." A shadow crossed Susan's bright little face. "My activities will be curtailed somewhat, and I was thinking . . ." She broke off to eye her guest a little apprehensively.

Vinney's smile was encouraging. "Yes?" she said gently.

"Well, I already have a girl helping in the riding school who will eventually take over most of my work, but it's the show jumping contest which takes place next month here that worries me. Tim won't hear of me even sitting on a horse now and I'd entered for it with high hopes – I have a wonderful horse, you see. I was wondering if you would take my place," she went on. "You were one of the best riders at the school years ago and you certainly haven't lost your touch. I've seen you putting Prince through his paces. What do you say?"

"I really . . ." Vinney began.

Susan cut in eagerly, "I've all the layout of the course here and you can practise every day on Tim." She laughed and nodded her head. "Yes, I called him after my husband, that's why I know I'll be lucky with him. Will you, Vinney, please?"

Vinney stared at her gravely. "I don't know what to say. I'm awfully flattered to think that you have such confidence in me, but it's a great responsibility. Supposing I lose?"

"You won't," said Susan confidently.

"All right, I'll do it – but only because an expectant mother should be free of all anxieties."

Susan was esctatic. "You darling!"

"That remains to be seen," replied Vinney darkly.

She rode home filled with misgivings. Tim was a darling and, after taking him through his paces at Susan's request, she had found in him everything that went into the making of a first class show jumper. Even so, becoming involved in village life, something she had vowed not to do, was disturbing. What was the use of putting down roots if they had to be torn up again? Her father had been her refuge and her strength. Losing him, and the way that he had died, had left her hypersensitive, vulnerable to the point of being a sucker for any kind word or gentle approach. If only it had been possible to become closer to her mother! But she had been made of different material. She was hard and bright like metal.

After stabling Prince, she entered the house to meet her mother in the hall. There was no charming expression of candour on the older woman's face as she stood there slim and formidable in Vinney's eyes. Strange, she thought, that even face to face we still can't make any contact, you and I. Years ago, I've met you like this, in this same hall, on coming home from school, and always there has been this kind of embarrassed nervousness that I feel now. The uneasy feeling increased, for there was nothing she could say that was light and spontaneous.

"I believe you went to tea with Grandmother Brandon," said her mother. "How was she?" Grace picked up the car keys from the hall table. Her smile was coldly polite as she spoke, breaking the brittle silence.

"Much better," Vinney answered, borrowing her mother's impersonality. "I've reels of films taken of Aunt Phyllis in Malta and I'm going to hire a projector to show them to her. I'm sure Gran will enjoy seeing what kind of life her daughter had on the island. There are some beautiful shots of the island. Perhaps you would like to see them too?"

Grace gazed on a face sweet and pure in the sunlight filtering into the hall. Her tone of voice did not change. "I doubt whether I can spare the time just now. I'm on so many committees and things. I'm driving into Downsend for lunch to discuss a dance in aid of the spastics." A glove was eased over wedding and engagement rings. "I shall expect you to attend, and to give a generous subscription to the cause."

Which, Vinney thought, with a sudden rush of colour to her face, is precisely the reason why you're asking me to go. It was on the tip of her tongue to reply that she might not be able to spare the time to go. Then, embarrasesd by unexpected emotion, unable to voice the words, she retreated. Black waves of depression washed over her.

She said bluntly, "I'll write a cheque out now, if that's what you want."

The other glove slid on. The brown eyes did not lift to the

troubled face of her daughter and her voice was as smooth as cream. "As you'll probably be approached to do so at the dance, we'll leave it at that. Incidentally, thanks for the cheque for your keep – I do appreciate it. I want to give Denise the best possible wedding when the time comes. I must do my best for her. You understand?"

Of course, only the best for Denise. The memory of the words jarred with the inevitable twist of pain in its wake to Vinney's heart. Her own isolation was complete, but an inflexible will forced her to take it on the chin. All the same, it was imperative to get away from her mother right away. With a slight inclination of her head, she went slowly upstairs.

Downsend Town Hall, resplendent with its new face lift and interior decor, was not as Vinney remembered it. The white-porticoed entrance matching the gleaming white and blue façade was not the mellow stoned building of her youth. Why was it, she thought wistfully, that the mellow tones of youth were always garish and ugly when one grew up?

It was the night of the dance given in aid of the spastics. Everything had been arranged very swiftly because the Town Hall was fully booked up for months ahead and this Saturday had been the only night available for the dance. Vinney arrived with her mother and Denise knowing that she was going to hate every moment. She wanted nothing so much as that the dance would finish, leaving her free to seek the sanctuary of her own room. She would play her part, forcing herself to join in the conviviality and light chatter, knowing that she was also decorative, but her heart would not be in it.

The enormous hall ablaze with flowers was bright, warm and golden beneath crystal chandeliers that glowed richly on dark panelling. Many of the people flowing in had been asked because of the size of their bank balance, like me, Vinney thought grimly. She looked with interest at the crowd, was literally swept into the cloakroom and swept out again, to find herself on her own. Trained staff passed to and fro, the dance band assembled and gradually the colourful throng split up and glided away in twos.

She waved to Susan floating by with Tim, saw her mother dancing with Charles Trevira and was herself claimed by his son Peter. He was an excellent dancer, not as handsome as Nick but compelling all the same. He held himself well, but seemed oblivious of the fact that he held a pretty girl in his arms. But then Vinney was oblivious of him too as her eyes scanned the room for Nick's broad shoulders and dark head. He was there through a gap in the dancers talking to Denise. They were moving slowly across the room in the direction of the conservatories when Peter swung her past.

After that Vinney heard neither the music nor anything of the movement around her. A feeling of crisis brought a painful dryness to her throat that would have soon been dispersed had she been able to follow the couple from the ballroom.

It was warm and quiet among the plants and flowers and Denise moved provocatively in front of Nick to turn and gaze up at him smilingly as he closed the door behind him. The smile gradually faded as his eyes, narrow and cruel, held hers. His voice rasped with anger.

"What's this I hear about us getting married? I've been congratulated twice this last week on my intention to marry the beautiful Miss Brandon in the near future."

Her fingers caressed his lean, hard cheek, her voice was low and seductive as she leaned her slender silk-clad form against him.

"Poor Nick," she crooned huskily. "Would it be so hard to marry the beautiful Miss Brandon? I'm surprised to see you so angry."

"I'm not against marrying Miss Brandon. In fact I'd already made up my mind to marry her – but your friends seemed to have the wrong christian name."

She laughed. "You mean they're under the impression that you're going to marry Vinney? You've only yourself to blame for that, my pet. After all, you did have her at your house several times and you also took her out to dine."

"Too true. That's why I can't understand your friends confusing her with you."

She said slowly, watching him, "What do you mean?"

88

"I mean," said Nick deliberately, "I'm going to marry your sister Vinney. She doesn't know it yet, but she will."

Denise drew in a furious breath. Her nostrils dilated and she went pale. "Is this some kind of joke?" she demanded.

He smiled. "I can assure you I've never been more serious in my life. Which brings me to the reason for bringing you in here. I would be obliged if you will tell Vinney that you and I are not engaged and have never been engaged. And stop waving that damned emerald ring about! You know well enough that you cheeked me into buying it for your birthday when you were in Sri Lanka. There were no strings attached."

For a split second her hands clenched and her eyes burned in her fury. Her face had gone even paler and her voice had a snarl. "So this is your revenge for finding me with Peter Trevira that day! Well, I don't envy Vinney. She's only getting you on the rebound. You'll never get me to believe anything else. You fool, she'll never satisfy you. I know."

Nick refused to be rattled. "Really?" lifting a quizzical brow. "I'm quite looking forward to teaching her to, if that's the case – which I'm sure it isn't. And whatever you believe is immaterial to me."

"I wouldn't be too sure if I were you," snapped Denise. "Vinney won't marry you."

When the dance number ended, Vinney found herself on the edge of the dance floor near to the entrance to the conservatory. And before she could decide whether it was by accident or design on Peter's part, Denise came out with bright flags of colour on her cheeks. She looked furious, but controlled her temper admirably as Peter asked her for the next dance.

"Please, Denise," he pleaded. "I haven't danced with you yet."

He stood there irresolute, waiting, while she gave him a long, provocative look. The light shone on her thick, luxuriant hair, on the thick eyelashes masking the brilliant anger in her eyes, and her red lips parted on pearly white teeth.

"My dear boy," she began, "I haven't danced with anyone yet and I am not likely to since I have to rest my knee as much as I can." The emerald ring caught the light as she rested her hand upon his arm. "Tell you what, if you're a good boy I'll sit one out with you later."

Eagerly, Peter took her up on her promise. "When . . . how soon . . .?"

But Denise was not listening; she was taking Vinney's arm. "I must introduce you to our Spastics Committee," she said, leading her away. "They're making the draw tonight for the winning ticket. I hope I win it. It's fabulous, the latest Jag. I'd love to make everyone wild with envy!"

Vinney had a momentary vision of the girl at the cash desk at the hairdressers and her own haste in signing her own book of tickets before hurrying away. Then she forgot the incident on a sudden wave of compassion for the luckless Peter. Denise, it seemed, was introducing her to all and sundry while making a beeline for what seemed to be the cream of the Spastics Committee standing by a small table at the entrance to the ballroom. There was a touch of recklessness about her that puzzled Vinney, who had been surprised to see her emerge from the conservatory without Nick. Something had happened between them, obviously, for Denise was gripping her arm painfully and she was actually trembling.

The next moment she was pushed forward with hard hands, and Denise was saying, "Here she is – the girl with all the money. My sister Vinney."

Someone spoke, a tall, expensively dressed woman whose hands were covered with rings. She was middle-aged with a long sallow face and big teeth which have her a horsey appearance.

She gushed. "I remember your father – such a handsome man. You have his eyes. It was a noble way to die. You must be proud of him." Her eyes, bleak and unsmiling, added, "But not proud of what you did."

Vinney flinched and Denise cut in easily on a distinct purr. "You mustn't embarrass my little sister. It was all so long ago and she was only a child at the time."

Her voice, louder than her usual tones, seemed to fill the room. With burning cheeks Vinney noticed other people joining their little group and staring at her curiously. Under their scrutiny her head reeled, their faces crowded in, became disembodied, leering and cruel. She wanted to run like a wounded animal to its lair. Then someone's hand was on her arm where Denise's had been. Nick's head and shoulders were shutting everyone out.

"My dance, I think, Vinney," he said, and led her away.

Nick moved with a slow comforting rhythm. The sensation of warmth and floating was balm to her pain. She wouldn't think. The ache inside her became a sweet pain that could only be assuaged by the feel of his arms around her. She wanted the reassurance of his firm lips against her own and her fingers curled around his. She drifted.

"I love you," he said.

The voice and the words bit into her subconscious. "What did you say?" she asked, startled and wide-eyed.

"I love you," he repeated. "I'm mad about you. Do you know that?"

"How can you? You don't know me very well?"

"My heart knows you only too well. It's thudding away there in thick deep strokes because I have you in my arms." He drew her closer against him. "Can you feel it beating?"

"Yes . . . yes, I can." She felt choked. "But a heart can be wrong, especially when it's allowed to rule the head."

His handsome face was arrogant, his lips moved in a mocking smile.

"It's no use, my lovely. I'm hooked for life," he was whispering above her ear, and she reached out for reality.

"What's Mac going to say about that?" she asked.

"What's Mac got to do with it? I'm marrying you, not him."

"Mac is your friend. Please let me be your friend too, Nick. It's all I can handle at the moment," she pleaded.

"You mean you don't love me?"

"I can't answer that, because I honestly don't know."

He swept her out from the dancers without a word and before she could find her breath they were drifting through open french windows on to a terrace. She was still in his arms and his head was shutting out the star spangled sky. The kiss was a long, shattering one, leaving her dazed and shaken and whispering agitatedly against his lips.

"Please, Nick," she begged. "This isn't fair. Besides, it's wrong."

"What's wrong about it?" His lips slid down her neck to kiss the hollow in the base of her throat.

"I . . . I told you . . . I wasn't sure."

He lifted his head and looked down into her eyes in a moment's pregnant silence. "You mean there's someone else?"

"No, of course not! I . . . I came home for a purpose and nothing is going to stand in my way. Not even you!"

Vinney drew a deep breath. In that moment she hated Denise for what she had done to her. She stared at his lean, dark face, hating also the barrier looming between them, a barrier of pride and endless nightmares.

His face darkened. "I don't care what plans you have or to what purpose you're holding me off. You and I were meant for each other and nothing you say is going to make any difference. You understand?"

He gripped her shoulders and looked down grimly into her pale face. For a despairing moment Vinney thought he was going to resort to violence and shake her hard, and fear whipped her to breathlessness. A soft evening breeze, sweetly perfumed by nocturnal scents from the garden, was all around them, moving tendrils of her golden hair, wafting her loveliness towards him.

Her eyes pleaded. "Nick . . ."

His eyes burned down into her and she attempted to move her shoulders out of his grasp. It was a mistake, but it was too late to stop the anger in him. Hauling her into his arms, he kissed her savagely, then he let her go.

His lips thinned cruelly as he spoke. "Actions, my sweet, speak louder than words. Your tongue might lie and say that you don't love me, but your lips don't. Try forgetting me if you can."

Someone came out on the terrace. Vinney felt bruised and battered. She could not look at Nick, but she had to turn to face the intruder. It was one of the waiters hired for the occasion.

"Excuse me," he said politely. "I came to tell you that the draw for the prizes is about to begin."

Susan and her husband Tim were the first couple she saw on entering the ballroom and she joined them, followed by Nick.

"Everyone's sweating on winning the car," Susan confided conspiratorially. "It's super. Can you imagine it, a hundred and fifty miles an hour red Jag, air-conditioned, centrally heated and almost soundproof inside. And all of nine thousand pounds!"

Tim said, "The tickets in my dear wife's tight little fist almost amount to that."

Susan flung him a dirty look teasingly. "You'll soon change your tune if we win it!"

Tim grinned. "I'm glad you said 'we', because if we did win it I'm afraid I shall insist upon driving it. The thing's much too powerful for you."

Susan snorted. "That's what you think!" she said darkly. "If I can handle a horse I can handle a car. I'd show you."

"Tim's right," said Nick. "A leaping monster like that would be lethal in your tiny hands."

Susan looked at him reflectively. "You males are all alike! Of course, you're dishier than most, but you still don't know a thing about women."

"I doubt if I ever will," was the pleasant rejoinder. "But I'm willing to learn."

They all laughed then at Susan's small wolf whistle and the draw began. There were lots of prizes, ranging from holidays abroad for two to bottles of wine. The draw for the main prize, the Jaguar, was being kept until the last. Vinney had not brought her tickets with her. They had been tossed forgotten in her dressing table drawer. Denise won a beauty case, but the other winners were strangers. When the draw for the final, most important prize began there was a breathless hush. The air, fresh and sweet, wafted in from the garden through a half opened window and Vinney felt an urge to go out and take a deep gulp of it. Thank goodness the evening would soon be over. She turned and met Nick's deep, absorbed gaze. He had been watching her enchanting profile and now his eyes captured her own. Vinney teetered . . . retreated a little and went pale as their eyes clung. She fought against the spell of his magnetism and was flung back to reality by a sudden murmuring among the gathering. No one present, it seemed, had the winning ticket. Among sounds of disappointment there were whispers coming from the platform where the draw was taking place amid the rustling of paper. Someone was looking through the counterfoils.

Suddenly the Mayor, who was making the draw, declared triumphantly that the winner had been found. The winner was Miss Vinney Brandon. Would she come forward? Vinney, disconcerted, put her hand to her face, felt it burn like fire and gasped, "Oh no, it can't be!"

She was aware of Susan hugging her, of a sea of faces all turned in her direction as the crowd parted down the middle to let her through. Pale as a statue and with an air of youthful dignity that sat well on her slender form, she walked to the platform to receive the keys of the car and a kiss from the Lord Mayor. It was the cue for a burst of applause from everyone present, and the row was deafening. Other men leapt on to the platform to kiss Vinney's flushed face and she was swamped by men.

"What about selling your kisses?" one smart alec shouted before he was rudely brushed aside by Nick. Vinney saw his dark hair tousled, his eyes blazing as he rescued her.

"I'll come with you to collect the car tomorrow," he said grimly.

The dance was over, Vinney back in her room was beset by conflicting emotions. Winning the car had added to her problems, but it was what she needed to travel about in. What if she was a target of jealousy? If the worst came to the worst, it was there to put the miles swiftly between her and her tormentors. As for Nick, she loved him with everything in her and dreaded meeting him again. Sooner or later there would be a showdown between them. Could she send him away, perhaps back to Sri Lanka, without her?

What did she want most, herself vindicated in her mother's eyes? Or Nick, who still thought her responsible for her father's death? She sat motionless on her bed in her evening dress and wrap, her hands clasped together in her lap. If it was to be a choice, her whole being cried out for Nick. The very thought of him filled her with a terrible nostalgic yearning. But she wanted to marry him free of any stigma. It wasn't difficult to imagine how the past would return to taunt her. When they had children to curb in their disobedience . . . your mother was disobedient once, with tragic results. Not that Nick would be so cruel, but the thought would be there in her own mind. How would she know that it wasn't also in Nick's?

There was a discreet knock on her door and Denise entered. She was limping slightly and sat down into the nearest chair with a grimace of pain. Her hand was on her injured knee.

"This knee of mine is playing me up after dancing." Her fingers massaged it slowly in a circular movement. She looked tired but very attractive as she flung back her head to show a white column of throat. "I haven't come for sympathy. I've come for a little chat."

Vinney said coldly, "You do choose your moments, don't you? What about tomorrow at breakfast – or don't you want to be seen talking to the black sheep of the family?"

The delicately pencilled eyebrows lifted insolently. "Why so touchy? It seems to me that being the black sheep pays dividends – first Aunt Phyl's legacy, now the Jag." The brown eyes narrowed into pinpoints of malice. "They say good luck comes in threes, so what's your third bag . . . Nick?"

Vinney refused to be baited. "You tell me," she challenged evenly.

"You love him, don't you?" demanded Denise.

"That's my business."

Denise went on massaging her knee and looking at her with something akin to hate in her eyes. "I saw your face when he acted like the gallant hero rescuing you from the mob. However, don't let it worry you, because Nick is crazy about you at the moment. He even asked me to tell you that there was nothing between him and myself." Tongue in cheek, Denise watched the result of her words on the small, pale face.

Vinney slowly relaxed from the tautness of her anger.

Nick loves me. He must do if he's admitted it to his ex-fiancée. The proof of his love was like a draught of heady wine flowing through her veins like fire. Her cheeks were the warm pink of a rose, her eyes deep blue pools of beauty.

"Don't look so love-struck!" Denise's voice ripped through the quiet room. "I don't know what Nick has told you, but I'm sure he hasn't mentioned how close we once were and that we would have been married now if it had been left to him. Why do you think he's stayed here for so long?"

Vinney's head lifted. "He came to settle his uncle's estate. You said yourself that he'd come over unexpectedly and found you with Peter Trevira."

Denise laughed. "I admit that. Don't you see that he's taking you on the rebound to assuage his pride, as it were? Our Nick is very proud. He also doesn't forgive easily, which is why I'm working around to that end."

"Good luck." Vinney looked her squarely in the eyes. "And now, if you don't mind, I'd like to go to bed."

Denise swung her foot to exercise the injured knee. "Why didn't you tell me you were taking Susan Ryder's place in the show jumping contest at Downsend?" she asked idly.

"I don't see that it has anything to do with you."

"Didn't Susan tell you?"

"Tell me what?" asked Vinney.

"That I'm riding too. It's about the only thing I can do well since I hurt the knee."

Vinney said, "I'm sorry about your knee. I hope it soon rights itself. But I can't see why it makes any difference to you whether I take part in the event or not."

Denise shrugged carelessly. "It doesn't, since I shall probably win. I've always beaten you in everything before." She laughed. "I suppose you think I'm conceited."

"Does it matter what I think?" wearily. "I take it that we shan't be the only two competing in this event."

"Oh no. But none of them, with the exception of Peter Trevira, will put up a very frightening performance." The brown eyes narrowed calculatingly. "Mind you, the horse you're riding is an unknown quantity. It was sired by a marvellous show jumper."

"I'm sure you won't lose any sleep over that," said Vinney. "Nice to feel confident and sure of winning. I'll have to try it myself."

"Do." Denise stretched her hands above her head and yawned before rising slowly to her feet. At the door, she paused. "Too bad I aim to win both events – Nick in the marriage stakes and the show jumping event too!"

CHAPTER SIX

THERE had been frost during the night and it glittered on the trees like tinsel as the sun came out. Vinney was glad the day promised to be fine with the tingle of early spring in the air. This morning at twelve o'clock precisely, the Jag she had won the previous evening was to be presented to her by the Lord Mayor at the car showrooms in the village. The outfit of her choice, a heavy cream jersey, a suede skirt and long suede boots, was to be offset by a soft, nylon fur loose coat.

Nick appeared on time and on her way down Denise was waiting for her in the hall. She was wearing a smartly tailored suit in her favourite cinnamon brown with a gay yellow scarf at her elegant throat. With the same unexpectedness she put on a smile, warm and friendly.

"You look like something out of *Vogue*," she remarked, dispelling the illusion. "I'm going to feel a tramp beside you."

Vinney stood still on the bottom step of the staircase. Something unpleasant, she felt, was coming. It was the first she had seen of Denise that morning and she was now ready for going out.

She said bluntly, "Why, where are you going?"

"With you to recieve the Jag. I couldn't think of you going alone."

"I'm not going alone and you know it. You also know Nick's car is at the door." Vinney started to walk across the hall. "Isn't that the real reason for your eagerness to accompany me?"

"One of them," was the smooth reply. "Come now, don't be so churlish. I want to help you to enjoy all the envious glances when you receive this king of cars. I hope you won't refuse me a ride in it." The coquettish smile curving her red lips was still in evidence when they emerged from the house.

"Good morning, Nick. Nice of you to take us," she said, sweeping forward in front of Vinney to greet him.

He straightened lazily from leaning back against the car and raised a quizzical brow. "The pleasure is all mine," he murmured, and opened the door of the car.

Denise hung back as he did so and Vinney slid into the back seat as her sister smiled up at him.

"I'll sit in front with you, Nick," she said in a voice as smooth as cream. "We must let Vinney arrive in isolated splendour, mustn't we?"

"Must we?" he answered, and slid in beside her to turn his head towards the back seat. "Got your car keys, Vinney?" he asked quietly.

"Yes," she replied, and her eyes collided with Denise's in the car mirror. "I can drive, you know. I've my licence with me."

"Good."

Nick said no more but gave his attention to his driving. Denise, however, had no intention of remaining quiet. She talked incessantly during the journey about her visit to Sri Lanka.

"You made my visit there a memorable one, Nick," she gushed. "I'll never forget how you carried me all that way to your house when I hurt my knee. It was so thoughtful of you to want to spare me the longer journey to the hospital."

Nick said bluntly, "As the doctor was dining that evening with my partner, Mac, my house was the obvious place to go. How is the knee?"

Her sigh was one of resignation. "I have little sleep with it, but then I have to bear it. The doctor does say that it's much better than it was and that, with a little more rest, there's no reason why it shouldn't be as good as ever."

She continued with a spate of bright determined chatter. The conversation, empty and meaningless, except as a means of shutting Vinney out, seemed to go over the head of the quiet man at the wheel until they reached their destination.

A murmur ran through the little crowd awaiting their arrival as the car drew up by the car showrooms. The Lord Mayor was there wearing his chain of office and Vinney recognised the members of the Spastics Committee. The red Jaguar sports car was pure luxury from the back bumper to the impressive headlights at the tip of the six foot six inch bonnet. There were murmurs of admiration as the Lord Mayor sang its praises before handing it over to Vinney. The press were there to take pictures for the local paper, and Denise pushed herself into several of them. Then Vinney found herself in the front seat with Nick sliding in beside her. The car leapt away like a streamlined predatory bird and she looked round for Denise.

"Where's Denise?" she asked curiously.

"I don't know," he said coolly. "Posing for more pictures, or I'm not Nick Wentworth. How that girl loves publicity!" They sailed over the hump-backed bridge in the village and people turned their heads to watch them go. "Did you ask her to come with you?"

"No. But she is my sister."

"When it suits her."

Vinney glanced at his profile and wondered how much he had thought about Denise. She was a very attractive girl, skilled in the art of playing up to any male, and Nick was very much a male. They had left the village far behind and were now running between cultivated fields and the occasional farmhouse. He was handling the powerful car superbly, but she was longing to have her own hands on the wheel.

He might have guessed her thoughts, because he said, "When we reach the motorway I'm going to let her out. Later, you can take over. Think you can handle it?"

He glanced down at her hands in her lap. Like her wrists, they were beautiful and delicate with a strong flexibility when holding the reins of a horse, as he had seen. She looked fragile, though her character was strong, sensitive too, and troubled over some particular problem which shut him out. But she was sweet and without guile with a gay humour crushed for the moment by trouble. Her beautiful dark blue eyes were deep pools of innocence, but she was warm and tender, passionate and chaste. The delicate perfume of her beat his blood to sudden heat and he knew he was in love for the first time in his life, so in love that it was damned painful.

They had lunch at a wayside inn, all oak-beamed and

latticed-windowed, where the food was all home-cooked with nothing out of a tin. There was a small vase of spring flowers on the table. They had wine, which made Vinney feel gay. Nick was sitting opposite to her looking into her eyes, intent and vital in tender concentration. Everywhere was romance. Vinney drifted.

He had let her take the wheel of the Jag when he had introduced her to all the gadgets. It had a push-buttoned life of its own and she was soon in love with the way it clung to the road like a lover. She had gurgled with joy when she let out the collapsible handbrake operated by pulling an automatic lever through a black slot. She had swept past the scenery like a bird purring around corners and sharp hairpin bends with confidence and skill. The countryside flashed by, green and sweet with the tender young shoots of spring, as new as the Jag, and her heart had sung. Everything hurtful and cruel had been left behind, with cows looking innocently on as they passed.

It had been coming up to two o'clock when she drove to the inn set in a valley of green fields and trees. Had there ever been a time when she had felt so happy? "Well done," Nick had said, and her heart had sung. Now she watched him as he ate his lunch. His hands were well shaped, the long fingers a masculine brown. His eyelashes were dark against the tan of his face and she longed to run her fingers through the crisp dark hair. A wave of tenderness swept over her leaving her breathless and her heart raced.

Am I wrong not to accept what the gods offer? Her thoughts mocked. Trust should go with love. Either you love him or you don't. If you do then you're a fool to hold back, a fool to be afraid to grab your happiness while you may. Her heart said wearily, you've gone over all this before and here you are again, considering a compromise instead of going on with what you must do. She thought of Denise, who would be more set against her now that she had the car and Nick's company.

Nick, looking up from his plate, unexpectedly caught her gaze. "Enjoying it?" he asked with a grin.

A warm feeling rushed up through her body and into her face. I love him so much, she thought. It would be so easy to give him everything he wants. Embarrassed at being caught staring, she stammered, "Yes, I'm . . . I'm enjoying it all very much."

"Where to now?"

They were back in the Jag after the excellent lunch and Nick was behind the wheel.

She said without hesitation, "Home, of course."

He looked startled. "Why?" he demanded. "The day is young, and what a day it is! Just look at that sky!"

Vinney stiffened in her seat. He was hurt and bordering on anger, she knew. The sky was an eye-watering blue, or was it the sky making her eyes prick with tears? All she knew was that, wherever one travelled, one was never free from the rest of the world. Already it was crowding in on them in the quiet valley.

She said, "I have to get back. I'm riding Susan's horse in the Downsend show jumping events soon and I'm due at the riding school this afternoon to practise."

"Don't they allow you any afternoon off? Like today. Isn't this something special? After all, one doesn't win a nine-thousand-pound car every day of the week. Besides," Nick grinned, "you're out with Nick Wentworth, remember, the fellow who's head over heels in love with you."

Desperately, she said, "You forget Denise still wears your ring. Everybody in Downsend is expecting you to marry her. I know Mummy is."

"So what? The ring means nothing to me. Why should I want it back? Good heavens, don't you trust me?"

He turned in his seat and gripped her shoulders. His mouth had thinned and he was furiously angry, so angry that she doubted whether he noticed her trembling.

She whispered unsteadily, "Of course I trust you, only . . . can't you see . . . you're rushing me?"

"Rushing you?" He frowned savagely. "Is it too much to ask that we become engaged?"

Her laugh bordered on the hysterical. "Oh, Nick! Two sisters wearing your ring?" Suddenly she sobered and pleaded, "I shall be in an intolerable position."

"Vinney," he said thickly, gripping her arms so hard that she winced, "what about the intolerable position I'm in, this . . . this ache in my arms that want to hold you when you're not there, this frustrating, tormenting agony when you're here, yet still unattainable? I know you have this thing about something you have to do, but what's more important than our love for each other? I know you love me – I saw it in your eyes just now at lunch. Why hold back? Don't you want to get married and raise a family with the man you love? What are you afraid of? Me?"

Vinney shook her head despairingly. His impassioned plea was battering down her defences. She was like wax in his strong hands and she had never come nearer to giving in than at that moment. But it was weak to do so when she had an aim in life – to do what she had to for her own peace of mind – and have the strength to do so.

A tear rolled down her cheek and he groaned and buried his face in her hair.

"Oh, heavens, Vinney, not tears! Let me kiss you better."

He proceeded to kiss her with long, determined, possessive kisses that frightened her, kisses that said, "You're mine and it's useless to fight against it."

And because she was frightened of her own capitulation, she managed eventually to push him away.

"No, Nick. Please take me home," she insisted.

He frowned and stared at her as though she was a difficult mathematical problem that he was trying to solve. The arrogance and tenderness arising from it had gone from his dark face, leaving it bleak and empty. His eyes, narrowing harshly, pinpointed her pale face.

"Don't you like my kisses?" he demanded. "Is that it? You don't love me?"

The words came of their own volition through stiff, cold lips. "I . . . I do . . . but I would like to go home now. I mean it."

A muscle moved in his cheek. "You're not going yet. I don't believe you have to go back to the riding school this afternoon. Susan won't expect you back so soon."

His arms were now only round her loosely and she knew it was impossible even to think rationally with him so close. She freed herself and his face set.

"You don't care if I marry Denise or not, do you?" he said with hard eyes. "She hasn't been very nice to you, has she? Nor your mother. Why don't you marry me to have your own back for their treatment of you? Not that I'd have you that way. One of the reasons I love you is that you've no vices and you haven't a malicious bone in your body. Come on," cajolingly. "Give me a kiss and say you'll marry me because you love me."

But Vinney was staring at him wildly. "How did . . . you know Mummy and Denise had been offhand with me? Someone must have told you. Who was it, Susan?"

He shrugged wide shoulders. "Does it matter? For one thing, I felt an atmosphere that first evening at your house, and I know you're very unhappy."

Her lips felt numb and they hardly moved. Each word was forced between them, "Then you know why. My mother hates me for what I did to Daddy."

"And Denise? Does she hate you?" he asked quietly.

"Denise and I have never got on together. She's always been Mummy's favourite," she admitted reluctantly.

"And she's jealous of you?"

"Does it matter?" she answered wearily.

"I'm trying to find out what really does matter to you." Nick gave her a long, searching look. "Vinney," his voice was a caress, "let's get married by special licence. Let me take you away from here back to Sri Lanka with me. I promise you won't regret it. You can trust me. I'm crazy about you, and it isn't a temporary phase that will pass. I'm stuck with it for the rest of my life." He was drawing her to him as he spoke, then he was kissing her with all the passion he had controlled for so long. He was vital and loving, murmuring against the insistent pressure of his lips.

"Please, darling, say you love me."

He had slipped his hands beneath the loose nylon jacket and his fingers were moving persuasively over her back. Their touch was electric through her sweater.

"I love you, Nick," she admitted.

For a moment she was blinded by the passion in the dark eyes meeting her bemused ones and he laughed softly. Passionate moments followed, their lips assuaging their hunger for each other. All Vinney could do was to cling until his feelings were once more under control as he grew tender.

"And you'll marry me soon?" he demanded softly, drawing her closer, his tanned cheek against her flushed one.

Vinney thought, if only this moment would last for ever! But such moments of ecstasy are short-lived, and panic shortened them further. Pushing him away, she said incoherently, "I can't marry you, Nick. Don't ask me to. I just can't . . . I love you more than anything else in the world . . . I always will . . . but I can't marry you." Her eyes filled with tears and he stared at her in bewilderment. "Let's go back. There's nothing to be gained by staying here."

"Suppose I say we're not going until I know what this is all about?" Nick said forcefully, and went to take her into his arms again.

"Leave me alone!" Her voice had risen, bringing slow anger to his eyes. "I want to go home. Don't you understand? I don't want to marry you."

"All right, you've made your point." Nick turned to the wheel and set the car in motion, his face grim. Then began the ordeal of silence, the numb feeling inside her as she saw the speedometer clock up the rate of travel and the final relief when they reached the car showrooms again.

"Take care when you drive home," Nick said as he slid from the Jag to pick up his own car. "Don't forget you're wielding a powerful weapon."

The coldness of his voice struck a chill to her heart and with a brief salute, he was gone.

Her mother was leaving the house when Vinney stepped from the Jag. She thought dismally, this is how I'll remember her for ever, going in the opposite direction.

As usual, Mrs. Brandon was beautifully groomed. Her dark hair was a smooth cap and her make-up no more than a glow on her clear skin. Vinney thought, her eyes should glow too, instead of being cool and wary whenever they meet mine.

The smile stopped short of the brown eyes. "I see you've collected your car," Mrs. Brandon said coolly, moving towards it. "I didn't attend the ceremony of handing it over because I'm a member of the committee and I decided it was politic to stay away since a member of my family had won it."

It might have been the painful encounter with Nick and the fact that her mother added uneasiness to her emotions already battered and bruised that prompted Vinney's rejoinder.

She said bluntly, "I'm sure your absence was unnecessary, Mummy, since everyone present knew that I'm the last person you would have wanted to win it."

The brown eyes had narrowed and were cold. "That was quite uncalled for, Vinney. I don't mind your winning it – although it certainly is far too powerful for a girl to handle. I hope you drive carefully. One tragedy in the family is enough."

Vinney flinched. "I think that last remark was uncalled for too, Mummy. You don't have to remind me that when Daddy died I lost my best friend." Her voice was not quite steady, but her mother did not soften.

"Didn't we all?" She peered inside the Jag at the push-buttoned splendour and lifted a graceful eyebrow. "I suppose it does wonderful things. You must take me for a run some time. I'm on my way to Grandmother Brandon." The pause was deliberate and pointed. "To tea." The dark head turned slowly from the car and Vinney waited. "It seems your visit brought out a human streak in her."

Vinney's throat felt dry and she swallowed painfully. "Grandmother is a lonely woman. Haven't you visited her before?"

"No – she preferred it that way. Your grandmother never forgave me for marrying her son."

Vinney considered this and said, "But you're family, just like Denise and myself. We're all she has left."

"Which is no reason for me to go where I'm not wanted."

"Grandmother wouldn't have invited you to tea if your visit

would be unwelcome . . ." Vinney began, and broke off as her mother walked to the garage for her car.

Slowly, she walked into the house and made her way to the kitchen. Sandy was there, washing the dishes after lunch. Vinney perched on a corner of the beautifully clean kitchen table.

"Sandy," she said, "have you any idea where I can hire a projector for some films I have?"

Sandy dried the last of the dishes and began to put them away. "No, I haven't." The cups were hung on their hooks on the Welsh dresser, then she turned thoughtfully. "The only person I remember having one is Colonel Wentworth."

Vinney, after carefully considering this, said carefully, "You're sure there's no one else?"

Sandy shrugged. "I don't know of anyone else." She picked up oven gloves and opened the cooker door to release the pleasing aroma of freshly baked scones. "Why not telephone Mr. Wentworth? I'm sure he'll be only too pleased to lend it to you."

Vinney slipped from the table and Sandy put down the batch of golden brown scones.

"Thanks, Sandy," she said on a bright smile which faded immediately into a frown at the telephone in the hall. Ignoring it, she she made her way thoughtfully upstairs to her room. It would be a mistake to contact Nick if she wanted to avoid further complications. She would ask Susan the next day when she went to the riding school to put Tim through his paces.

But her enquiries the next day failed to produce any results. Susan had sent her to the rambling old vicarage, now a youth club since the vicar had moved into a smaller place which was less expensive to run. Vinney explained her mission to the caretaker, who shook his head. "We had one, but it's broken. Colonel Wentworth up at the Manor had one. I can't say for any other."

Towards the end of the week when further exhaustive enquiries failed Vinney was discovering that it was one thing to make decisions and quite another to live up to them. It wasn't possible to avoid Nick indefinitely in a small village. They were bound to meet some time, but they had to be casual meetings when it was possible for her to keep her emotions tightly locked up.

The trouble was that even the thought of Nick left her breathless. She wanted him so much. She longed to ask him to help her, to seek forgetfulness in his arms, to let him know that she was warm flesh and blood like him and equally capable of passion. Would he marry Denise in the end? She hoped not. He would not be happy with Denise. She was too spoiled, too fond of having her own way.

That weekend was one of heavy rain and dark skies. Sandy went down with 'flu, then Mrs. Brandon and Denise followed suit. It seemed there was an epidemic of it around. Vinney was the only one to escape unscathed, and she looked after the three of them. It was hard work, but in a way much more enjoyable than having nothing to do. The doctor called. He looked tired and fed up and Vinney heard him giving a round of abuse on the drive when his car refused to start.

He came back to the house to use the phone. "Nobody does a decent job these days," he grumbled on his way to the telephone to call up the garage. "It's only a matter of weeks since I had the car overhauled and now it's gone again."

"Take the Jag," Vinney said generously. "You can keep it until your car is made serviceable again. I'll fetch the keys." She was back quickly to see. He was still standing there with a look of wonderment on his tired face.

"But it's a new car and an expensive one at that. Are you sure?" he asked.

Vinney took his hand and put the keys into it. "There you are. You're welcome to it – honestly."

"I don't know what to say," the doctor told her after she had taken him to the car to explain the gadgets. "You're too kind."

Vinney returned the grateful pressure of his hand and said, "You don't happen to own a projector, do you? I have some films which I want to show to my grandmother."

He shook his head. "I'm sorry. The only man I knew with

one locally was Colonel Wentworth from the Manor."

Vinney drew in a tight breath and clenched her hands. "If anyone else tells me about Colonel Wentworth owning a projector, I shall scream!"

Instantly, the doctor's fingers were professionally on her wrist. He timed her pulse and frowned. "You've been doing too much," he said. "You want to take it easy for a couple of days. I hope you're not going down with the 'flu."

"I'm sorry," she murmured contritely. "But everyone tells me about Colonel Wentworth, and he's dead."

He looked at her searchingly. "But he left everything to his nephew. You have only to ask him."

Vinney blessed her sudden high colour. "I know that . . . but he might not have it now." The excuse sounded terribly weak and she mustered a smile.

He smiled. "You can soon find out. Ask him." He patted her arm. "And look after yourself. Keep your patients warm with plenty of hot drinks. I'll call again – and thanks for the car."

The next few days were hectic with everything to see to while looking after three invalids. Vinney marvelled how Sandy managed to get through all the chores with just a daily woman coming for a few hours in the week to do the washing and cleaning. By the end of each day she was too tired to change from her slacks and cashmere sweater. Sandy had been very poorly, having refused obstinately to go to bed when she was first off colour. But Denise had been the most demanding. By the time they were all on their feet again, Vinney was exhausted. A house with illness in it is never a happy one at the best of times, and the first time the patients dressed and came downstairs was not much brighter. Vinney had packed them all off to bed early and they had been more than ready to go. She had been aching to have a hot bath and go to bed herself, and was about to do so when the front door bell chimed. Uneasily, and resenting whoever the caller was, Vinney raised a hand wearily to a face without make up and hoped for the best.

"Nick! For heaven's sake, it's ten o'clock! What do you

want?" Her voice betrayed her irritation and to some extent her embarrassment, for her appearance in the slacks and sweater put on that morning was anything but fresh. And her head throbbed.

"Do you really want me to answer that truthfully?" he mocked. "I could, my sweet, only you would slap my face and shut the door before I could ask how you were."

He towered above her. Her heart somersaulted just to look at him – to have him so near, smiling down at her mockingly. She wasn't sure if her sudden giddiness was due to him or her tiredness.

Her lips moved and her voice sounded strange in her ears. "I was just going to have a bath and go to bed. Are you coming in?"

He came in and stood with his back towards her as she closed the door. For fleeting seconds her heart was in her eyes, loving the back of the well-shaped head topped with crisp dark hair that her fingers itched to touch.

He said, "I saw the doctor just now in your car. He told me your family was down with 'flu and that you'd lent him the car while his was in dock." He turned round slowly to face her and Vinney dropped her gaze to stare down at her clasped hands.

"So you called to see how Denise was?"

Nick was silent for so long that her head was compelled to lift and her eyes faltered at his brown throat. He was looking down at her intently. She could feel his eyes but had not the courage to look up at them.

"I could have called for any number of reasons." He came to her through a mist of tears. "Would you have minded if I had called to see Denise?"

Vinney bit hard on her lip to stop it from trembling. Her thick lashes lowered in an attempt to stem the tears.

"Where are you going?" this as she made an attempt to walk past him.

"I'm . . . I'm going to make a hot drink for the invalids. I promiseed to take them a nightcap anyway," she answered numbly. "Perhaps you'd like a drink."

"Vinney." His hand was on her arm, the fingers strong and standing no nonsense. Her name on his lips was music to her ears and she was in his arms without knowing how she got there. She was in a vacuum of ecstasy, Nick's lips hard and sweet on her own. For several moments her brain was incapable of thinking clearly. It was like a drug which she had craved for, but, like a drug, forgetfulness of her worries was only temporary. This was what she had been afraid of, this weakness to cling instead of holding him off.

Nick's deep voice was murmuring in her ear with a strange thick break in it. "My darling, why fight? I told you I could make you mine."

The masculine arrogance of his words brought her back to sane reasoning, where she was and the reason for being there – all that Denise had done to her and what everyone, including Nick, believed her to be, a child whose disobedience had caused her father's death. Falling from such shattering emotional heights, Vinney was in no condition to come to terms with Nick. What had happened to her during the last ecstatic minutes must never happen again until she had done what must be done. There must be no more weakening in her resolve, no more giving in to the demand of her heart which, she realized with humiliation, was far too easy to obey.

Wrenching herself free from his arms, she forced words through her lips. "Please, Nick, leave me alone. You're spoiling everything," she cried piteously. "You're . . . too demanding. You . . . you take possession of me until nothing else matters, and . . . and that's wrong. It isn't for me."

His arms had dropped as he saw her face and he made no further attempt to touch her. Instead his dark eyes pierced down into her unhappy ones.

"My sweet," he said gently, "that's what love is all about. We're in love with each other and you know it. You're struggling against something bigger than yourself, bigger than both of us. So don't play with me. I want you and I mean to have you. Whatever bee you have in your bonnet about any obstacle looming in your girlish mind you can forget here and now. The outcome will be the same, no matter how you struggle against it. Do I make myself clear?"

"Perfectly."

The voice came from the doorway. Denise stood there in a wrap that showed every seductive curve of her body. Between brown lashes, her eyes gleamed vindictively. Her smile stopped short of the hard look in them, but her voice was as smooth as silk. "No wonder you didn't hear my bell, Vinney! I rang for that nightcap you promised to bring upstairs. I wouldn't mind if it was something important holding you up." She glided across the room to look up provocatively at Nick, and shook her head. "Such a waste of time, my dear Nick. Vinney will never marry you – I told you before."

Vinney flitted from the room like a slim, pale ghost wafted away on the brittle laughter from taunting lips.

"What would you like to drink?" Denise moved seductively towards the drinks cabinet.

"Nothing, thanks," sharply.

Winged eyebrows shot up, beautifully manicured fingers, pink-tipped, curled around the bottle of sherry. "Oh, come now! Surely you aren't going to take it out on a poor little convalescent? On my first day up too. Incidentally, thanks for the lovely bouquet I never received." The glass filled, Denise raised it to her lips and smiled at him over the rim. "Fortunately, I had some rather wonderful ones from Peter Trevira."

"I thought you'd asked Vinney for a hot drink. Why the sherry?" Nick asked brutally.

Denise was extremely amused. "I decided I didn't want it. Sit down and let's be matey."

"Women! I'll never understand them. Goodnight, Denise. Don't get drunk. There'll be no one to carry you to bed." Nick strode to the door and her taunting voice followed him.

"Why not stay and oblige?" she suggested archly. "You carry me so beautifully. You're so strong."

The bang of the front door was her only answer and, gliding to a sofa, Denise reclined gracefully upon it with an arm draped along the back to sip her drink. Had Vinney seen the look on her face she would have been extremely worried.

CHAPTER SEVEN

THE days overlapped each other and Vinney drifted through them in a state of lethargy. Everything was back to normal again at Brown Thatch, except that her mother was a trifle more kindly disposed towards her. Not that it made much difference to Vinney, who began to keep out of her way now that she was up and about again. It was a break to go to the riding school to put Tim through his paces once again, and she loved the atmosphere at the house with Susan wallowing in her state of pregnancy, like 'a contented cow' – to quote her own words. Her own feeling of loneliness was emphasised by the complete togetherness of Susan and Tim. To her way of thinking there was nothing in life as wonderful as loving and being loved.

She had known that life would be empty without Nick, that every waking minute in which she did not see him would be filled with an aching longing, but it did not help. Vinney knew how wrong she had been to even think it would be so easy to turn him away. And there was still that terrible memory of the past that would always catch up with her and give her nightmares. She forced herself to be gay and uncaring, finding plenty of activity to take her out of herself by taking over some of Susan's chores at the riding school to help out.

Life took on a more exciting slant as she made more friends among the pupils there and their families and her social life became hectically gay. There were dances, birthday parties and invitations galore and she became a popular addition on invitation lists. Walking in on Denise one morning, on arriving home for lunch, she found her standing in the hall leafing through the midday post.

"Two for you," Denise volunteered, proffering two envelopes towards her without looking up.

Vinney accepted them and went slowly up to her room. Her heart was pounding when she recognised the very masculine scrawl on the top one, which bore a local postmark. It was from Nick, an invitation to a housewarming to be given on the evening before the Downsend Annual Show Jumping. Bits of gossip from time to time about the progress of the workmen at the Manor had come to her like crumbs to a starving person's table. Now it seemed they had all moved out, hence the housewarming.

The thought of seeing his dark, brooding face, of feeling the reassuring clasp of his firm brown hand gave magic to the very air she breathed and heaven seemed very near. Then, as though to cast the spell of his magnetism aside, she threw the letter down and picked up the other. It was from her grandmother, asking when she was going to visit her again now that the 'flu epidemic had gone.

"I know that is one of the reasons you kept away, in case you brought the germ to me, and that you've been very busy nursing your family," she had written. "However, it does seem an age since you came. Please come soon."

Feeling rather guilty at not calling to see the old lady, Vinney gave a deep sigh of resignation. Moments ago, torn as she had been between wanting badly to go to Nick's party and the wisdom of it, it had been ten to one against her going. Now the decision had been taken out of her hands. The promise to show her grandmother the films taken in Malta could only be kept if she could procure a projector for the job. You can't ask Nick about it and turn down his invitation at the same time, common sense argued. Accept, and ask him while you're there.

They walked through the great arched doorway of the Manor to meet Nick, who stood in the bright golden cavern of the hall where flower arrangements were set brightly against dark panelling. Golden velvet curtains cascaded to the floor from beneath fringed pelmets gracing the tall windows and crystal lights brought to life ancient shields and sabres on panelled walls. Modern decor, skilfully applied, relieved the solemn grandeur of a passing gracious age. So thought Vinney, glancing through an archway into the lounge.

"Congratulations, Nick," said Grace Brandon as they stopped before him. "I like it very much."

Denise murmured, "What it is to be rich!" while Vinney, behind them, looked at him beneath her lashes. The golden light gave his clear-cut features a teak tanned look and his teeth gleamed as white as his shirt front. How wide his shoulders looked in evening dress and how well his dark arrogant head was set upon them. Then he was greeting her, and she was afraid of the cold, merciless gleam in his eyes. Or was it a trick of the light? It could have been the latter because, as their eyes met, he smiled mockingly to bring the heat to her cheeks. She murmured something and made way for the next arrivals.

The dinner and the wine were excellent, with Nick as the perfect host. Vinney tried to ignore his presence, but the dark head a little to her left over a bowl of roses imprinted itself upon her mind. Somehow his vibrant personality came across to her and she was overconscious of his nearness. Her mother and Denise were seated opposite to her between Charles and Peter Trevira. Watching the two men engrossed in their table companions, Vinney wondered if the seating arrangements had been made with future romances in mind. Her eyes wandered from them to collide with Nick's, who was watching her. Could he read her thoughts? Her face grew hot beneath the mockery of his eyes as she smiled then looked away.

Susan, seated beside her, whispered mischievously, "I'm eating far too much and I'm sure Tim is ashamed of me. He keeps giving me a nudge each time I spoon out helpings from the silver dishes. I'm sure he forgets I'm eating for two!"

Vinney laughed. "Go ahead. Wait until he sees that bouncing boy you're going to produce!" Her eye caught Tim's on Susan's other side and he winked. Her smile was sweet, as she winked back. Lucky people, she thought, so content with each other.

There was dancing later in the music room to a radiogram. Nick did not join in the dancing. He was much too busy seeing that his guests were being attended to. Vinney was enjoying herself and was flitting in and out of the dancers with no lack of partners. The evening was going very quickly, as an enjoyable one has a habit of doing, and she still had not spoken to Nick about the projector she wanted to borrow.

The opportunity came between dances as she sat waiting for her partner to bring refreshments. Susan and Tim weren't far away. Susan was attacking a cream cake, and Tim was laughing. His expression was saying, "My darling wife, if you eat much more you'll burst!"

Vinney chuckled.

"Pleased to see you happy." Nick was there looking down at her with a trace of mocking humour.

Her heart tilted. "It's a lovely party, Nick. I'm sure everyone here is happy," she said.

"And what about the host? Do you want him to be happy?"

The quizzical lift of dark eyebrows, the lines of his lean dark face and slowly curving, mobile mouth all served to quicken her heartbeats. Take care! Retreating inwardly, she assumed a lightness of tone and kept her voice steady.

"Aren't you?" she teased.

"I could be happier. For instance, what's Tim got that I haven't?"

His intent gaze was on her and it was useless to try to evade it.

"I don't understand?" she answered evasively.

"I saw the exchange of winks at dinner and just now you were looking tenderly in his direction," he accused evenly.

She laughed. "Just a joke we were sharing. They're so happy together it's a tonic just to see them. They're nice people."

"I couldn't agree more." He sat down in the seat awaiting her partner. His dark gaze, now faintly ironic, made her feel uneasy. "Jealous?" he asked.

Vinney nodded.

He leaned forward, dangerously near, and said forcibly, "Then why hold me off? Why the blazes don't you marry me? I can soon put you in the family way, if that's what you want, and we can all be happy."

Vinney lowered her eyes. "I've been wanting to ask you something all evening," she said.

"Yes?" He smiled.

"I believe the Colonel was interested in photography and that he had a projector. If you still have it, may I borrow it?"

Nick's smile vanished. His mouth curved in bitter humour and he rose indolently with loose-limbed grace to his feet. "I have and you may," he answered laconically. "And now, if you'll excuse me, I must see to my guests."

For a moment the dark eyes held her own and the look in them made her feel suddenly breathless. Then he was gone.

Later, Vinney was taking her leave with her mother and Denise when Nick detained her with a light touch on her arm.

"When do you want the projector?" he asked coolly.

"I wanted to show my grandmother some films I have at her house. Do you want me to come and fetch it?"

His fingers were sending electric tremors up her arm. Vinney knew she had hurt him and she stood with agonised immobility unable to do a thing about it.

He did not smile. "Will Thursday suit you? I can deliver at your grandmother's."

Vinney managed a smile. "That will do fine, thanks," she replied.

"It's going to be nice for the Show tomorrow," her mother remarked as she drove home to Brown Thatch. "Are you sure you'll be all right, Denise, riding with that injured knee?"

"Don't fuss so, Mummy," her favourite daughter said irritably. "Of course I'll be all right. I hope you're right about the weather."

The evening air was filled with the faint, chill sweetness of early summer. Through the partly opened car window, Vinney felt it caressing her hot cheeks. Somehow the customary after-the-party conversation going on between her two companions seemed irrelevant and apart. It was a relief to know that Nick would take the projector to her grandmother's house – at least it did not involve their meeting again. The thought made her feel more desolate than ever.

"What's this about a projector?" Denise broke in on her thoughts and turned in her seat beside her mother to cast a baleful eye on Vinney. "I suppose it's another scheme to further your acquaintance with Nick. You never give up, do you? It won't be a bad idea for us all to tag along on the night in question. Really – first the doctor, now Grandmother Brandon! You are ingratiating yourself, aren't you?"

Because Vinney's nerves were already on edge, Denise's voice rasped across them painfully. A sick feeling gripped her and she said tonelessly, "As it happens, Nick is the only one who can help me regarding the projector. As for ingratiating myself with anyone, you know it's not true. I lent the doctor the Jag because his own car broke down on our drive and he had more calls to make that evening after calling to see you."

Her voice faded into a brittle silence and no more was said before the car turned into the drive at Brown Thatch. They were all three walking indoors when Denise said silkily, "Are you still determined to ride in the show jumping contest tomorrow?"

Her brown eyes taunted and she smiled, a dangerous and enigmatic smile, which Vinney refused to let rile her.

She nodded. "Yes, I am."

"Pity. I shall win."

But Vinney had already gone towards the stairs and up to her room. She was trembling as she shut her door in spite of her determination to keep cool beneath her sister's jibes. The moonlight streamed in through the window and she moved across to it. How much longer must the nagging ache in her heart go on? There was so much hate in her sister's face, and she herself was not one to hate. That challenge thrown at her like a gauntlet, contemptuously, and with utter confidence had touched a hidden spring inside her. She would take that challenge. Until now riding Tim in the contest had been more or less as a favour to Susan, her friend. She had hoped to win for Susan's sake. Now it had become more than that. She had to win for her own sake, to prove to Denise that there were times in life when even she would not get all her own way. In the past, Denise had bettered her at every turn, done it maliciously and contemptuously. Well, she wouldn't this time!

The Show had begun in the morning beneath a cloudless blue sky. The huge marquee had been toured by the judges before lunch to consider the prizes for the usual exhibits. Mrs. Brandon, flushed and smiling, had been awarded first prize for her flower arrangement and had won several more prizes in the cookery section. Vinney congratulated her as they walked to the refreshment tent for coffee. Denise, she noticed was with Peter Trevira, who only had eyes for the mocking face lifted so provocatively to his. Of Nick, she had seen nothing.

The show jumping was scheduled for three o'clock that afternoon, and Vinney felt a shiver of excitement feather across her skin as the time drew near. The sun blazed down on the pretty dresses and masculine attire of the crowd with no sign of Nick. Then she saw him near to the paddock and moved hastily away.

He saw her and strode across the short, springy turf to touch her arm.

"Hello, Vinney," he said quietly. "Nervous?"

Her chin lifted. "No. I'm going to enjoy it," she replied with spirit. Her dark blue eyes shone with purpose and he watched them narrowly, respect mingling with something else that churned her heart.

"Riding or winning?" he grinned, and the white of his teeth lit up his lean, sardonic face.

Her heart reached out to him, whipping her into breathlessness. The faint breeze, perfumed by crushed turf and flowers, moved the rich honey gold of her hair, bared her slender white throat. It seemed the most natural thing to do to walk into his arms. Her limbs stiffened, but her smile was bright. Steady, my girl. Watch it!

"Both," she answered.

"That's the spirit! Here come two of your rivals for the cup."

Nick was looking over her head as he spoke.. The next moment Denise and Peter Trevira joined them. The two sisters, contrasts in colouring, were alike and elegant in their well-cut riding clothes. Vinney wore a gold sweater; her skin gleamed like a warm ripe peach beneath her golden hair. Denise wore her favourite cinnamon brown with a bright green scarf tied around her slim throat. She was superbly confident with a dark-eyed magnetism that flowed from her in waves. Her eyes beneath the thick fringe of brown lashes gleamed with a frightening intensity. Vinney looked the more relaxed with a quietness of purpose in her dark blue eyes. Her youthful dignity sat well on her slender shoulders.

Watching her, Nick knew that he had been completely bowled over by a girl for the first time in his life, and the fact that she was making herself unattainable maddened him to distraction. He lighted a cigarette. His life had run along pleasant lines. His easy, good-natured tolerance had made him popular with both sexes. His friendship with his partner, his all-absorbing work in Sri Lanka had been enough along with the breaks in between, visiting the old country or going off on a fishing trip. Women had merely been a distraction from the normal routine. They were mostly all the same, decorative, seductive and more than willing to give pleasure. Not one of them had done more than cause a slight twinge in the region of his heart. Never for a moment had he considered the possibility of meeting someone who would blow all his theories about women sky-high. He would have scoffed at the idea that somewhere there was a soulmate deliciously designed just for him. But not now. Right here in this lovely sun-washed meadow was the girl who held his future happiness in her small, slender hands. If only he could make her believe that nothing mattered except the fact that he loved her and always would!

Peter Trevira was the first contestant, and he rode out to the starting point, a fine figure of a man on his horse. Vinney kept her fingers crossed for him. She liked Peter. He had a kind of wistful smile, and she pitied him too for being in love with Denise. There was the usual last-minute hold-up that kept his horse pawing the ground, impatient to be off. Vinney looked wistfully over the sunlit scene, the colourful hats of the spectators in the enclosures, the old oak trees that had stood guard for generations around the course. Here the inalienable beauty and charm had been preserved and tended lovingly for generations.

To Vinney, with the brilliant colouring and clarity of light and shadow of Malta in mind, there was something inexpressibly dear and restful in the gentle green countryside, the rolling hills and the cool air coming in from the sea. A murmur ran through the crowd and Peter was off. There was no hesitation with man or beast; both rode as one, and Peter made a clear round. The applause was deafening. Then it was the turn of the second rider, a pale rather nervous-looking young man who worked at the local bank. He had four faults.

Denise was next to the last just before Vinney and she rode magnificently. Vinney caught Nick's eye and she laughed with sheer exhilaration when he saluted her with a grin. Tim trembled as they moved off to the starting point and she leaned forward to pat him steadily.

"You and I are going to have fun," she whispered in Tim's cocked ear. "You, my pet, are going to enjoy it as much as I shall. So here we go!"

And they did. The next to the last jump, deep, rough with a brook to clear – a nasty place to land in – gave Vinney a few qualms. Then Tim was sailing over to make a perfect landing. A low murmur of voices sprayed over them. Vinney was smiling now and swung Tim round gently for the last jump. He whinneyed with pleasure, his hooves bit into the turf, and she felt his buoyance as they sailed over the top. It had been a clear round, beautifully done.

The crowd were loving it. Now it was between Peter, Denise and herself – two to be eliminated for the final winner. It could be any of them. Vinney caught Susan's eye as Peter rode towards the starting point. She had been chattering away to her husband and she blew a kiss. Vinney smiled in return and Tim raised his hand. A low murmur of sympathy went up from the crowd when Peter scraped the top of the third jump. He finished with one fault.

Vinney was next. Giving Tim a friendly pat, she ventured forth and let him take over. He was completely relaxed, with the memory of the last enjoyable canter still fresh in his horsey mind. They were sailing on a pink cloud – at least, it seemed so to Vinney who perspired a little as they approached the brook. The next moment he was over the top. There was dead silence while she turned him round gently to the last jump – then it was over. Tim had given a beautiful performance, and the crowd went wild.

Denise rode up to the starting point. She sat her horse superbly and she was more familiar with the course than Vinney, which gave her an advantage. Outwardly she assumed an air of complete calm, but inwardly she was still recovering from the shock of Vinney's performance. She was breathing hard and her mouth was a thin pink line. At the fifth jump she grazed the top bar and looked furious. She spun the horse round and Vinney caught her breath. She had always been frightened of her sister's violent temper, and it showed now in the two flags of angry colour in Denise's white face. She landed well after clearing the brook and cleared the last jump. But the damage was done. Vinney had won!

The crowd cheered. There was wild applause, and Susan hugged her with joy.

"I knew you'd win!" she cried, and kissed the horse between his large soft brown eyes. "Oh, boy, aren't we going to celebrate? Vinney, you're a darling, and I insist that my husband shows his gratitude by giving you a kiss!"

Tim, of course, did not need any encouragement. His mouth, firm and warm, rested on Vinney's for several seconds. Then Nick was there.

"Mind if I join in the fun?" he asked. His dark eyes were grim beneath a forbidding frown.

Susan gurgled. "Certainly. You can come home with us. We'd planned a little celebration – I know it was rather premature, but you see, I knew anyone named after my husband couldn't do anything other than win."

Nick said dryly, "Lucky Tim."

It was all over. Vinney had the cup which she gave to Susan and they went to the car park. Mrs. Brandon's car had gone. She had seen nothing of Denise and neither of them had been there to see Vinney receive her prize. Vinney was worried.

Denise could be bitchy, and now she had a reason to.

"I'm taking you in my car," volunteered Nick.

She looked up at him, still disturbed. "I shall be expected to go with Susan," she said.

"That's all right." Susan's eyes twinkled. "Nick is coming, so he can bring you."

Nick put her in his car and swung out on to the road. Vinney sat silent beside him.

"Happy?" he asked, flicking her a keen look.

"Naturally," she answered.

Sarcastically, he murmured, "Don't bubble over, will you?"

Her smile was a pale one. "I'm sorry." Her voice was toneless. "I suppose it's the aftermath of all the excitement and strain. Have you seen Denise?"

He frowned down at her, his dark eyes pinpointed in puzzlement. Vinney felt his rising anger. She was not enjoying the victory over Denise. Now it was all over it was not hard to see the extra problems her victory could bring. Her sister would be against her now more than ever. But her ego had been severely dented. At least there would be no more crowing over herself on Denise's part. It was small comfort. However, Nick must not be dragged in at this juncture. It was necessary for her to be alone for a while to think things out.

"Denise has gone off with Peter Trevira," Nick told her. "Are you upset because you beat her?"

Vinney thought this over and admitted honestly, "I wanted to at first. Now I'm not so sure."

"Why aren't you so sure? What's Denise got to do with it?"

He's upset, she thought. He could be taking me on the rebound. Denise still has his ring and he hasn't bothered to get it back. Oh, why can't one read people's thoughts? Life would be much easier. Anyway, I don't want any more trouble at the moment.

Impatiently she said, "Let's forget it, shall we?"

They were nearing the riding school, with Tim and Susan driving ahead.

His voice was dangerously deep. "You and I have got to

have a long talk together, and the sooner the better. I refuse to be put off any longer. I'm dining out this evening, but I'll see you at your grandmother's house tomorrow night when I take the projector. Will anyone else be going?"

"Denise might be there, and Mummy too," Vinney told him.

"Then we'll have to arrange something else, shan't we, if they get in the way?"

Susan and Tim stood waiting for them as the car slid to a halt. The sun glinting on the silver cup in Susan's hands was no brighter than her eyes. She was in high spirits. Thank goodness somebody is, she thought darkly.

It was high tea with lashings of champagne. Besides Nick and Vinney, there were a dozen guests, friends of Susan and Tim. They all sipped champagne from the cup and everyone was in high spirits. Nick left early for his engagement that evening.

"Come and see me off," he whispered urgently to Vinney.

They walked in silence to his car, Vinney on the defensive and clinging desperately to a neutrality that he could crush as easily as a flower beneath his well shod foot. She was aware of him looking down at her, but she had no intention of looking up at his face. It was impossible though to ignore the brown lean hand swinging at her side. His magnetism came across to her in waves and it occurred to her that he had captured scores of feminine hearts without being aware of it. It was obvious that he was now out to capture her own. But the past was a wall through which she was still seeking a door, and until that door was found and opened they were for ever divided.

He paused with his hand on the door of his car. "Feeling any better?" he asked sardonically.

She quivered under dark eyes that questioned, at the set jaw and grim mouth. Her voice was suddenly desperate. "I wish you'd leave me alone!"

"I can't. You might as well tell me to stop breathing." His mouth twisted in a smile that did not reach his eyes. "Is there . . . another man . . . someone you left behind in Malta?"

Surprise, not guilt, shone in her deep blue eyes. Her head moved from side to side in denial. "No one."

He said unbelievingly, "You mean to say there was not even one man who wanted you in marriage, looking as you do?"

She laughed, loving his jealousy. "There was one," she admitted.

He frowned darkly. "Who was he?"

"Someone who was after my money."

"You're joking!"

"No, I'm not."

"Was he the only one?" His expression had lightened, but he still looked grim.

Vinney looked right at him. "He was."

Nick grinned. "I believe you, although I find it hard not to. You must have had admirers – no, listen." He lifted a hand before she could speak. "I love you. I didn't want to love you, it just happened, and it's damned painful. You stepped right into my heart and there's no pitching you out. I love everything about you, your sweetness, your lack of vices, the clear, forthright way you have of looking a person in the eye when you speak to them, your innate honesty and compassion."

When he would have touched her, Vinney drew back dithering between an overwhelming joy and deep despair.

"It's . . . it's . . . no use," she stammered. "It wouldn't work. Please go."

For what seemed an eternity, he stared down into her working face and his jaw set.

"Tomorrow evening at your grandmother's house. I shall be waiting for you." He uttered the words like an ultimatum and before she could gather her scattered wits, he was gone.

Later she fell to wondering if he knew where her grandmother lived, and then called herself all kinds of an idiot for not realizing that Denise had probably introduced him to all her family.

CHAPTER EIGHT

THE first thing Vinney did the next morning before going down to breakfast was to look out the films Uncle Paul had taken in Malta. They would bring back nostalgic memories for Grandmother Brandon when she saw her daughter coming back to life on the screen. But they were films of happy days, in fact the happiest Vinney had ever spent in her life. Had she been wrong to come home and leave all her friends in Malta? This was her home, but did she really belong here at Brown Thatch?

A cold hand seemed to squeeze her heart as she became aware of what little progress had been made since her arrival. Her mother was no nearer to accepting her as a daughter than she had been ten years ago. Now things would be worse since Denise would blame her for her failure to win the show jumping event the day before.

When the opening of her room door broke in on her thoughts she looked up fully expecting to see Sandy enquiring when she was going down to breakfast. Instead it was Denise who cast a comprehensive glance at her fondant pink fine cotton trouser suit on entering the room. She was wearing an Italian house gown in golden brown and orange silk etched with blue and her thick brown hair hung in a heavy braid over one shoulder.

Her smile was surprisingly pleasant. "Sandy wants you to come down to breakfast. She's cooking bacon and eggs and seems to think you're not eating enough."

Her glance at the case filled with films was curiously oblique. Vinney, surprised and touched by Sandy's concern, had no immediate answer to that one. She straightened, snapped the case shut and watched her sister stroll to the dressing table to pick up a cut glass scent spray.

"Not bad," was her comment as she sprayed the perfume behind each ear. Her voice was as smooth as silk. "By the way, Mummy and I have decided to go with you to the film show at

126

Gran's this evening."

Her voice was far too casual and Vinney swallowed on a dry throat. Weeks ago the announcement would have given her great joy with the warm feeling of togetherness with her family that her heart craved. Now it did little more than fill her with a vague apprehension.

"I hope you enjoy it," she said.

Denise put the scent spray back on the dressing table and considered her for a few moments. "You don't sound very enthusiastic about it?"

"I'm surprised, that's all."

"You mean after yesterday?" Denise shrugged. "I'm not childish enough to hold the fact that you won against you. I'd underestimated you in your prowess in that direction. It will be interesting to see the films." The brown eyes narrowed into slits as she leaned back against the dressing table. "I take it you're on the films too?"

"Yes. But it's the ones with Aunt Phyllis on that prompted me to offer to show them. Grandmother Brandon has seen nothing of her daughter in all the years of her marriage to Uncle Paul."

Denise shrugged again carelessly. "That was her own fault. Aunt Phyllis married a Maltese, didn't she, against her mother's wishes?"

"I think Gran's sorry now and she's awfully lonely."

"And you're going to perk her up. Haven't got her money in mind, have you?"

Vinney's face flamed. "That's a beastly thing to say! I'm going down to breakfast."

She marched out of the room and ran lightly down the stairs to meet the pleasing aroma of bacon crisp and brown from the pan. Sandy was shovelling it out along with two eggs on to a warmed plate.

"Come on, Miss Vinney, see what you can do with this. I'm quite proud of you winning that Cup yesterday. They say good luck comes in threes. You won the car, then the Cup. I wonder what the other will be."

She went to the kettle already on the boil and made the tea, and Vinney sat down at the table. Sandy's kind words were balm to her after the spite of her sister, who didn't come down to take the edge off her appetite while she ate. To her surprise she enjoyed her breakfast. Later, when Sandy had left the kitchen on some errand or other, she washed the dishes, put the crockery away and went to telephone her grandmother to tell her about the family going that evening after dinner to the film show.

Feeling the evening would be soon enough for another session of her sister's company, Vinney went out in the Jag, now returned to her by a very grateful doctor with an outsize box of chocolates, for the day. Her destination was a market town where she had lunch and spent the day looking round the open air stalls and the lovely old mellowed rows of shops which formed the High Street. It was one of those balmy summer days with no wind, and heat in the sun, and she enjoyed the outing enormously.

There was only the three of them for dinner that evening. Denise was quiet and watchful, giving Vinney the idea that she had been the subject of their conversation while she had been out earlier that day. Consequently, she found it hard to relax in their company. Her mother began the conversation by asking where she had spent her day. She told her. Since her return home there had been little opportunity for any long conversations with her mother and it was distinctly strange to be chatting with her now, a little maddening, too, because she was so uncaring. It was a relief when they didn't linger after the meal and all trooped out to her car for the short run to Grandmother Brandon's.

Nick was waiting for them at the door to take the case of films from the car. It was still early summer and in the fading light he looked wide-shouldered and strong, his dark suit fitting his long leanness like a glove. If he was surprised to see the three of them his white smile hid the fact admirably. Vinney thought his glance rested longer on Denise than on either herself or her mother.

The soft warm light greeting them when they entered the room was from the open fire place of burning logs. The drapes at the tall windows were drawn together and Grandmother Brandon sat in her usual chair with cushions at her back. The firelight gleamed on the low table and the silver coffee service. Nick had evidently had dinner with the old lady and they had drunk their coffee in the lounge. In turn, they all went to kiss her soft cheek dutifully and settled down in chairs nearby. Nick had fixed up the screen, and as the housekeeper came in to remove the coffee tray, Vinney went across the room to explain about the tapes.

"These are the early ones," she explained. "Uncle Paul took them just after he and Aunt Phyl were married."

Picking up a roll of film, Vinney handed it to him. He scarcely looked at her as he fixed it in the projector. He worked quickly and confidently. She knew he was under the impression that she had deliberately brought her mother and Denise along to avoid a tête-à-tête with him. She was annoyed herself that it had to be him with the projector. So if he was annoyed as well that made two of them.

The film was taken at the Villa Rosa and it unfolded to show her aunt, first as a bride very unsure of herself, then as a woman blossoming out in the knowledge that she was truly loved. That it had been a successful and very happy marriage there was no doubt. It showed on their faces and in their looks at each other. There were films taken at religious feast days with Uncle Paul's Maltese family where dark eyes under hooded lids gave an alien air to the colourful scenes of the beautiful island.

A second film of the children, relatives of Uncle Paul, was delightful with the introduction of Vinney who had arrived at the age of eleven an unhappy and bewildered child. She was a white and gold English flower among so many peonies.

Under cover of the conversation, Vinney said hurriedly, "Not that one at the beginning – cut it out. I forgot, it's mostly of me. Just show the end. There are some very good shots of Aunt Phyllis."

"So what?" Nick looked down at her hand on his arm. "I'm sure your grandmother will enjoy them. What is it you want to hide?"

"Nothing. Can't you see they're not interested in me? They want to see Aunt Phyllis."

He moved his arm and her hand fell away. "You're family too, aren't you?" he said acidly.

"It will open old wounds," Vinney hissed into his ear as he bent to do something at the projector.

"Wounds have a habit of healing cleaner when exposed to the air," he answered brutally. "Relax."

Vinney's hands clenched by her sides as the film unwound to show her on the beach just after her arrival in Malta. She was wearing her swimsuit and with the tragedy of losing her father still fresh in her mind, she was refusing to go into the sea. Aunt Phyllis, shapely and charming in her swimsuit, was trying to persuade her. Finally it was the swarm of Maltese children, small bodies brown as coffee beans, who carried her forward with them into the water.

It was apparently the beginning of a happy life for Vinney on the island. In between many beautiful shots of the island and many of Uncle Paul and Aunt Phyllis, Vinney was shown blossoming delightfully into womanhood surrounded by love. There were shots of her swimming like a seal under water with Aunt Phyllis and streaking along the beach in her swimsuit with her long golden hair flowing out behind her in the sun. Her long golden legs became familiar on the screen in shots Vinney had not seen before. In fact, she was beginning to realize that there were quite a number of the films she didn't remember seeing, or having been taken, for that matter.

Uncle Paul had been a pet with a bubbling sense of humour and it was just the kind of thing he would do to take pictures of her when she was unaware of him doing so. He had been probably chuckling when he had taken the one flickering across the screen now, for it was one she had never seen before. It showed her dining out with his nephew Bruno at a beach café in the shade of palm trees. Her head was bent, her thoughts completely absorbed in the food on her plate, too engrossed to see Bruno looking at her with his heart in his eyes.

Vinney broke out in a cold sweat. Poor Bruno! He must have

been in love with her and she never knew. She had thought that he had wanted to marry her for the estate Aunt Phyllis had left, but maybe it had been a bit of both. He had always been one for the girls. She could have been one of many.

Nick said, his voice a deep growl under cover of the conversation of the others at the other end of the room, "Who's the admirer? He looks ready to eat you."

"He was Uncle Paul's favourite nephew, Bruno."

"Is he the one you said was after your money?"

"Yes." Vinney bit on her lip. "Look, I've never seen this film before," she whispered hastily.

"So you didn't know the man was in love with you – or did you?" Nick was angry. It vibrated in the deep tone of his voice.

"I . . . I told you –" she began, when Denise cut in.

"What are you two talking about back there?" sharply. "Discussing our Vinney's love life on the island? She's a dark horse, Nick. You don't want to believe a word she tells you."

Grace Brandon was heard to whisper something inaudible in the irate ear of her favourite daughter and all was quiet. But the silence was ominous to Vinney, who felt her sister's jealousy as something tangible. She knew Denise was furious because Nick was with her some distance behind in the intimacy of the darkened room. There were waves of electric current warning of an approaching climax, and Vinney knew herself to be right in the centre of it. It was not made any better by Nick, who had become frigidly polite upon receiving the last roll of film for the evening. There were many more to be shown, but Vinney thought that ten o'clock was late enough for her grandmother to be up, especially as there was no knowing yet how she would react on seeing her daughter Phyllis come to life on the screen.

It was a little after ten o'clock when Nick had run through the last of the film and Miss Tatten came in with drinks and sandwiches to round off an entertaining evening. Then the old lady went to bed after thanking them all for coming.

"Come with me to my room, dear," she said to Vinney. "I want to thank you properly for being so kind to come and cheer up an old woman. Will you come again and tell me more about your life on the island with Phyllis? I missed so much, and I've been very silly and stupid."

Vinney promised, looking anxiously at her grandmother, who was now leaning heavily on her arm. Her face had a curious grey tinge. It wasn't until the old lady was tucked up in bed that her colour became more normal. Vinney sighed with relief, and when Miss Tatten came in with the usual nightly pill it was waved aside.

"Put it down for a moment and bring my jewel box," the old lady instructed.

The box was brought and placed on the bed and an ivory hand shakily drew out an exquisite silver bracelet set in stones of every hue.

Vinney bit hard on her lip, guessing the old lady's intention. "Please, Gran – if you're giving that to me, don't. I don't want any reward for just showing you a few films."

"My dear, it's not meant as a reward. It will give me great pleasure if you will accept it. I don't remember enjoying an evening so much for a long, long time. And that charming young man had me wishing I was young again." Her smile was suddenly mischievous. "Is he yours or Denise's?"

She laughed at Vinney's high colour and reached out for her hand to clasp the bracelet on her wrist.

"There," she said. "I won't bother you for an answer since it seems to embarrass you. I suppose time will tell. Enjoy my little gift – and now I'd like my drink. I'm very tired."

"You don't think it was too much for her?" Vinney asked Miss Tatten, who came downstairs with her after making the old lady comfortable.

The housekeeper patted her arm. "Your grandmother is all right, a little overtired perhaps, and no wonder. She's been talking about you coming this evening all day and she thoroughly enjoyed dining with Mr. Wentworth. I never heard her laugh so much. Do come again soon, it will make her very happy."

Vinney hesitated in the doorway when she returned to the

lounge, feeling very much like an intruder. Nick was lounging back against the Adam fireplace with a drink in his hand and the two women shared the sofa, looking more like sisters than mother and daughter. Denise was very glamorous in a strapless green evening gown from which her beautiful shoulders rose with the sheen of a pearl. Grace Brandon was in ice blue, a long-sleeved dress with a low-cut v-neckline at the back. They were talking together in friendliness and laughter. Seeing that a mask of spurious gaiety was called for, Vinney assumed one and entered.

Her mother was the first to speak. "How is the old lady? I hope the rehashing of the past wasn't too much for her."

Vinney sat down on a chair on the opposite side of the fireplace and looked across into her mother's bland expression. Were her words meant as a criticism of her own action in showing the films? Or was her concern for her mother-in-law genuine? Discomfort swept over her and she said quietly, "She's all right. I think she enjoyed it."

"I'm sure she did." Nick was putting a drink in her hand and his firm fingers brushed her trembling ones. "We all did. Sandwich?"

She shook her head at the plate he offered and he put it down. Then Denise was speaking.

"I'll have another sherry, Nick, and a cigarette." Brown eyes shone up at him provocatively as she offered him her empty glass. There was a far different expression on the face she turned to Vinney when Nick strode across the room to the sideboard. "I was a little disappointed at the show," she commented. "I expected to see more of your love life."

A chill feathered over Vinney's skin at the venom in the words. The hand raising the glass of sherry to her lips was not quite steady. What was this sister of hers up to now? She braced herself for what was to come when the silky tones underlaid with malice filled the room. "If that dark admirer of yours is anything to go by it was certainly something. Don't you agree, Nick?" Denise put a slim white hand on Nick's brown one as he applied a lighter to her cigarette. Then with a drink in one hand and the cigarette in the other, she leaned

133

back indolently to rake her sister's pale face with hard eyes. "What are the Maltese like as lovers? Do tell us."

Nick had gone back to his place by the fire. Vinney could feel the eyes of all three directed upon her, Nick's most of all. She went alternately red, then white, and was aware of the sherry burning its way into her stomach.

Her voice, when it came, was slightly husky from a thick apprehension rising in her throat. "Why not pay them a visit, then perhaps you can tell me?" she suggested without expression. All right, Denise, you've asked for it, she thought. "Of course, when I'm your age and have knocked about a bit, I might be able to tell you, but so far I haven't had your experience with men."

Two spots of angry colour stood out on Denise's face and her lip curled.

"Still playing the innocent, aren't you?" Her laugh wasn't pleasant. "Well, you can't fool me, if you can fool Nick. He wouldn't think you so wonderful if he knew you'd tried to blame me for Daddy losing his life in the sea all those years ago. Nick has no idea how crafty you can be, worming your way into Aunt Phyllis's affections until she left you all her estate!"

Her voice was suddenly harsh and ugly. This, Vinney thought, was one of her sister's rages that no one apart from herself and her mother had ever seen. There was nothing beautiful now about Denise's contorted features. Vinney flinched. She had always hated rows and had never been any good at slanging matches. In her opinion they were too degrading. Bewildered and helpless, she received an extraordinary vivid picture of Denise, her face drained of colour staring at the bracelet on her wrist. Vinney had forgotten it. Her sister, however, recognised it as a gift from Grandmother Brandon and she seemed to go berserk.

"There, you see! What did I tell you? Doesn't that prove that I'm speaking the truth?" Denise pointed her cigarette dramatically to the bracelet, which Vinney made no attempt now to hide. "Her latest spoils, a bracelet from Gran, one of the family heirlooms!" The brown eyes, glaring now with hate and malice, flung out a challenge to Nick, who was leaning indolently against the fireplace.

"Denise, behave yourself!" Grace Brandon laid a restraining hand on the shaking shoulder of her daughter. "All this is so uncalled for and very embarrassing, I'm sure, to Mr. Wentworth. The bracelet was your grandmother's to dispose of as she wished. As for Mr. Wentworth, I hope he'll overlook this . . . this outburst of yours, which I'm sure you'll be sorry for tomorrow. In the circumstances I think we'd better leave before you say something else you'll be sorry for."

Denise glared at her mother, her anger heightened by the placating hand on her shoulder. Then she turned on her suddenly, her face marred and twisted.

"And let Nick be hoodwinked by this Jezebel of a sister?" The words were spat from her mouth. She turned on Nick. "Can't you see what kind of woman she is? Just a mealy-mouthed wanton out for what she can get!"

There was dead silence in the room. Slowly the passion and anger faded from Denise's face at the look of distaste, and something more, on Nick's that made her squirm. Her teeth grated together. She flung the words at him.

"You fool! You utter fool!" she cried, and fled from the disgust that he made no attempt to conceal. The door slammed behind her.

Grace Brandon rose to her feet, pale as alabaster. "I must apologize for my daughter, Mr. Wentworth. She's a little overwrought. It never pays to dig up the past." Vinney's presence was ignored for the moment. "I hope you'll forgive her little outburst. It was all spoken in anger, so I trust you'll think none the less of her for it. Goodnight. We'll be waiting for you in the car, Vinney."

She swept by with scarcely a glance at the stricken figure sitting as still as a statue on the other side of the fireplace and the door closed behind her.

"Finish your drink."

Nick, bending over Vinney, spoke forcibly. The paleness of her face and the large dark blue pools of her eyes shimmered up at him, and caught at his heart. He had to restrain himself from taking her into his arms. But this was not the time. In his opinion, like Denise, she was beside herself too – not with anger and jealousy; it was something he could not describe, a kind of hopeless despair, and he would have to be stern to shake her out of it.

There was a secret of some kind she was keeping from him – he was sure of that. His hands, firm and strong, curled around her cold ones, lifting the glass to her lips and holding it there until it had been drained.

"I'll take you home," he said, putting down the glass.

Vinney shook her head. Her colour was coming back. She said, "We came in the Jag and we'll go back in it."

He followed her across the room with a stride, his fingers curling around her elbow. "I'll see you tomorrow. Where can we meet?" he asked.

"Nowhere." Her tone was expressionless. "I shall be at the riding school all day."

They were at the door and he pulled her round to face him. His eyes blazed and a cruel slant came to his mouth. "I said where can I meet . . ." He broke off suddenly and his whole demeanour changed as her extreme youth and unhappiness whipped him to soberness. He went on more gently, "Look, I know you're tired and upset, but I must see you tomorrow. You won't be at the riding school tomorrow evening. I'll call for you at seven-thirty."

Her protest was one of poignant appeal. "You . . . you can't want to see me again, not after what Denise said. It's no use, Nick."

He looked grim. "That's what you keep saying, and I want to find out why. Seven-thirty tomorrow night."

It was five o'clock when Vinney arrived home to Brown Thatch after a day at the riding school taking Susan's place in coaching the riders. No one was home and she took a bath. The day had been one she longed to see the end of. That morning a telephone call to her grandmother had assured her that the old lady felt no ill effects from the excitement of the previous evening. The news had taken a load from her mind, but the four walls of her room seemed to close in on her.

As she put away her riding clothes and slipped on a dress it seemed imperative for her to go out, to walk down to the sea and think things out. Snuggling into a cream woolly coat and thrusting her hands into the large patch pockets, she was soon walking disconsolately along the beach. The only thing she seemed to have done so far, ran her wretched thoughts, was to make things worse than they were. Denise would always resent her and her mother couldn't care less, so what was the use of staying? It was only common sense to leave, and the sooner the better.

A swift glance at her watch told her it was just after six o'clock, time to go back to the house and pack. With luck it was possible to be away before Nick arrived to pick her up. Sandy would be in the kitchen preparing dinner. It would be quite simple to say she was staying with friends for a few days and write letters when she reached wherever she was going. Vinney had not the courage to think beyond that point. Her mind made up, her footsteps quickened back to Brown Thatch – and there, barring her way, stood Nick. Her heart lurched sickeningly. It was quite an effort to pull herself together and speak lightly.

"You're early," she managed. "It isn't seven-thirty yet."

He said equably, "No, it isn't, is it? If it was you'd be miles away. Am I right?"

Vinney looked up pleadingly into his dark enigmatic face. "Don't you think it would have been better that way? It's no use, Nick. Denise has poisoned your mind against me, and it's only my word against hers."

"So what? Tell me your side," he said calmly. "Let's sit down, shall we? Here's as good a place as any where we shan't be disturbed."

He drew her towards a cluster of white boulders backing the beach. They were at the foot of the slope leading up to Brown Thatch, and he pushed her down gently on to a flat one still warm from the afternoon sun. As he lowered himself beside her Vinney put her head back against a backing boulder. The sea was calm and gulls sailed on the placid surface like scraps of paper. The soft evening mist was settling down gently over the scene until everything about them seemed unreal and far away.

Nick spoke first. "About Denise. Has she bothered you at all today?"

Vinney shook her head and continued to gaze out over the sea.

He spoke softly. "What was it all about? I can understand the gift of the bracelet triggering off a spark of jealousy, but what was all that about blaming Denise for your father's death? Was it all lies?"

She turned her head and looked at him and her eyes hardened. "Not really. I did try to put the blame partly on Denise, I did inherit Aunt Phyllis's estate and I did receive the bracelet from Gran. So what?"

Nick frowned heavily and his voice was clipped. "We're going to be married by special licence – I can get one within three days. I've two months of my leave still to go and we can spend them in a honeymoon in London or Paris, wherever you choose."

"You must be joking!" she gasped.

"On the contrary, I was never more serious in my life."

He leaned over her and took in the gold of her hair, the violet blue of her eyes, alluring eyes that a man could drown in, and his lips moved over the petal softness of her cheeks. When his mouth claimed hers, their hard insistency thrilled even while it terrified her. The magic seeped through and there was no resistance in her; only a complete surrender to a power stronger than herself. As she soared to heights of happiness undreamed of, it seemed to Vinney that the past had been obliterated, that only the call of the heart mattered. It was the soft wash of the surf on the beach, the mocking quality of it reminding her of the past and all its pain, that brought her back to reality. Passion died in her. Nick was whispering her name. He was ardent and demanding now. His lips were moving down into her neck.

"Let me go!" She fought against the arms holding her so strongly like a mad thing. Minutes ago she had been mad, utterly confused and unable to think clearly. Once she was out of his arms her mind would clear and it would be easier to do what she had to.

"Vinney! What's the matter? What is it?"

Nick glared down at her. His arms had slackened and at the look on her face, they released her altogether.

She looked up at him sadly. "Nick, this is all wrong. It wouldn't work. You must see how impossible it is. Neither of us can forget the accusations Denise flung at me last evening. You have no proof of who was speaking the truth. The only proof you have is the evidence which proves her words and which I have no means of repudiating. There would always be a doubt in your mind – you must see that."

His arms were creeping round her and he was suddenly warm and ardent again. "But I love you, my sweet. Marry me and let me do all the worrying." He drew her close, bending his head to kiss her lips, very gently.

Vinney shook her head on a stab of misery and stiffened in his arms. Her resistance communicated itself to him and he felt her withdrawal from the passion and warmth of his love. He frowned. If only he could glean even an inkling of the real cause of her behaviour! She was the faithful type, even to a sister like Denise, who had revealed herself as a bitch. He was sure of that, just as he was sure that she was not the kind of person Denise wanted him to believe she was. His first instinct was to carry her off and take her to his house until he could make her see sense, but that kind of drastic treatment would not work. There would have to be some other way to find out the truth.

He said, "You're fighting a losing battle, my sweet. I always get what I want in the end, and I want you." He gave her a smile which lighted up the sardonic expression put there by his thoughts. "It's just a matter of patience, something that a tea planter knows a lot about," he assured her. Then, more serious, "You will let me know if you're thinking of going away?"

She nodded. "I'm sorry, Nick. I love you, but it's a kind of unhappy love instead of being joyous and full of fun. I can't feel happy about it, although I know you're the only man who will ever count in my whole life. I love you too much to let you take an unhappy woman as your wife." Her lips trembled. "I'm going now. Goodbye, Nick."

Vinney had packed her cases when there was a tap at her door and Sandy entered. "I didn't hear you come in – " she began, then stopped short on seeing the packed cases. Her expression was bland and curious. "Are you going to stay with her?"

"Stay with who?"

"Your grandmother."

Vinney stared. "Why, is there anything wrong?"

"Then you haven't been to see her just now?" asked Sandy.

"No, I went for a walk. What's the matter? Is she ill?" Vinney's heart went cold and she waited with bated breath.

Sandy shrugged. "The housekeeper telephoned about half an hour ago to ask if you would go over as your grandmother wasn't well and was asking for you. I wasn't to tell your mother or Denise. Apparently it's only you she wants to see." She gave another look at the suitcases and her smile was droll. "I was thinking that was where you were going."

Vinney caught her eye and smiled. "It's an idea. Sandy, you're a darling!"

Miss Tatton looked worried when she admitted her into the hall. "I'm so glad you've come, miss. I'm afraid you've just missed the doctor – I sent for him because your grandmother has been acting so strangely in the last hour or so. She had her lunch as usual and her afternoon nap. It was when she woke up."

"Yes?"

Miss Tatton gave a deep sigh. "She'd obviously been dreaming, because she asked me if her husband had come in from the garden. Then she laughed, and said, 'He's hiding somewhere. I know he's here, because I distinctly felt him kiss my hair'."

Vinney swallowed on a lump in her throat. "Was that all she said?"

"Well, no. But when I gave her afternoon tea, I noticed that she could not hold the cup. Apparently she had suffered a slight seizure – the doctor confirmed it."

"I see. And where is she now?" asked Vinney.

"The doctor and I put her to bed. He says she must remain quiet. Only her right arm appears to be affected, but the doctor is convinced that the use will return in it. He's calling again in the morning." The older woman hesitated, then, "She's been asking for you. She appears to have grown very fond of you, and I was thinking if you would care to come and stay with her until she's well again, it would help her a great deal."

Vinney nodded. "Why not? Actually, my cases are in the car."

CHAPTER NINE

LIFE with her grandmother needed little adjustment for Vinney, who now found her days filled with helping out at the riding school and looking after the old lady. Most of the influences and emotions pressing down on her at Brown Thatch had been pushed in the background by the very different atmosphere at Four Cedars. She had been made to feel wanted and welcome. But there had been no word from Nick. Her mother and Denise had called on several occasions to see the old lady while Vinney had been at the riding school, but neither of them had made any attempt to contact her or show any interest whatever. Whether or not they had deliberately chosen to call when she was out did not seem to matter any more; the meeting would have been painful anyway. Sandy called once or twice with some calves' foot jelly she had made for the old lady, and commented on her departure that Vinney was looking less harassed and much better.

Then one morning Nick telephoned on a morning she was not due at the riding school. "How are you?" he asked, and went on without waiting for a reply. "Will you go out with me this evening? I've been very good not pestering you for a fortnight. But I can't deny myself the sight of you for another day. I promise to behave myself."

At the sound of his deep voice, Vinney felt her legs turn to jelly. How many times during the last fortnight had she ached for the sight of him, the touch of his hand and the comfort of his arms.

"Are you still there?" he asked.

"Yes . . . yes, I'm still here. I can see you, but it will be after nine o'clock when Gran has gone to bed."

Her breath halted in her throat at the pause that followed. So much better if he refused, common sense said. But her heart as usual did not agree. The last fortnight had been desolate without him and this was only the beginning. The years ahead would all be without him. Unhappy away from him, unhappy with him. Why not choose the latter while she could?

"A crust to a starving man," he murmured. "I'll pick you up at nine sharp, and bring a key. I'd hate to keep that nice Miss Tatton up."

He went on to ask about her grandmother with concern and sent his regards, saying he had been in London and had returned the previous evening. He had dined with friends who had told him about the old lady being ill. Mid-morning two bouquets arrived from him, one for herself and one for the old lady. They were hothouse blooms beautifully arranged with satin ribbon. Vinney put the flowers in vases and tried not to think of her date with Nick that evening. She had put the cards accompanying his flowers in her dressing table drawer, looking yearningly at his firm masculine scrawl as she did so.

As she glanced up into the mirror the unhappiness in her eyes gave her food for thought. For a girl who was going to meet the man of her heart that evening she was looking decidedly glum. Love to her had been an unknown quantity until Nick had entered her life. In his arms all that the poets had said about love had come true, with all the sweet torturing torment that ensued. There was no doubt of the overwhelming happiness life with Nick would give her, if only she dared take it.

The problem was how long was it possible to repulse him? To marry Nick, to truly belong to him, to know his tender teasing and the full measure of his love would wipe everything else from her mind at first. But what as the years went on? How could she ever be sure that he had really shrugged Denise's insinuations completely from his mind? If there had been the tiniest doubt in his mind that doubt could lie dormant until some incident happened to coax it into life. She had always been gentle and kind; it was her nature to be so. Would he in time misconstrue her actions, knowing how Denise had described them as being utterly different? It was a risk she could not take.

She was ready when he came on the stroke of nine. He

opened the car door for her, and conscious of him sliding in to his seat beside her, Vinney, who had willed her pulse to normal in the last hour, was sure that the heavy drumming of her heart must be audible in the confined space of the car.

A glance at Nick showed him to be disturbingly well groomed and dangerously attractive in evening dress. His greeting had been skilfully casual, but the look in his eyes when he set the car in motion told her that he would stop in some not far distant convenient place and have his own way with her. He did just that, stopping the car in a layby off the country road.

Vinney said a little breathlessly, "What have we stopped for?"

He turned towards her, his arm on the wheel, and gave her a tender mocking appraisal. "I want to look at you, to touch you, to know that you really do exist. However, I could do it much better if you'd look at me."

Vinney had lowered her eyes to the evening bag in her trembling hands. Now a firm but gentle finger touched her chin to turn her face up to his.

"Well, my sweet? Have you missed me?" he demanded.

Her cheeks were a warm rose. "Yes, I have."

"I've missed you like hell. Does that mean anything to you?" His arms were sliding around her slim suppleness, drawing her into the close circle of his arms. His head bent, shutting out the world and all her intentions to remain calm and uncaring. The kiss was one that had to make up for all his longing – hers too, only he must never know it, Vinney thought despairingly.

Those few ardent moments carried them both away from earthly things. She closed her eyes, wanting the kiss to go on for ever as her arms went up around his neck. It was Nick who drew back first with an unsteady laugh.

"A drink to a thirsty man," he murmured, placing his hard cheek against the deepening rose of her soft one. "You know I'll never let you go, don't you, my sweet? Am I glad I've found you!" More ardent moments followed while he kissed her bright eyes and soft throat. At last slowly, unwillingly, he relaxed his hold and put her back in her seat, tweaked the curl at her ear and turned to the wheel. "We'll have to go, my sweet," he said, and put the car in motion. "I've booked a table at the inn where we dined before. I hope you're hungry."

The car leapt to his bidding and shot forward through the dusk. The air had sharpened with the warning of rain in the offing. Vinney was sitting demurely beside him, her cheeks rosy from his kisses, leaning back in her seat and watching him with a stifled longing, loving him yet hating herself for being so weak. She awoke from her trance-like state on reaching the inn, which welcomed them with the warm of an open fire and cosy alcoves set with tables for two.

As the waiter showed them to their table, the fire, bright with flame against the dim wall lights, illuminated the room, showing up the teak tan of Nick's dark face, Vinney's flushed warm cheeks, flashed diamonds on the crystal vases of carnations on every table and caught the white teeth of the girl dining with her blond companion nearby. Denise, and Peter Trevira.

Fixing her glittering eyes on Vinney's faintly repellent look, Denise greeted them both in a hard brittle voice.

"Well, well, look who's here! Welcome to the Tavern. I see you're still fond of our old haunt, Nick," she said meaningly. "I thought you were in London."

"I was until yesterday," Nick answered in his slow drawl. Strange he hadn't noticed before how hard her voice could be and how it grated. Politeness forced him to add, "How's the knee?"

"Practically well again." The brown eyes were dark pools in a set pale mask of a face. "Do join us."

Nick's eyes narrowed down on to their table, saw they were at the coffee stage and declined politely, "No, thanks. I've already booked a table."

He exchanged a few pleasantries with Peter Trevira about the Boat Show in London while Vinney kept silent and fully aware of Denise sitting there with a cigarette in her hand smouldering no less hotly than the gleam in the veiled eyes. How she hates me, she thought, and smiled at Peter as Nick steered her to their corner table.

If Nick noticed her subdued mood as they ate he did not mention it. He talked easily about the shows running in London, declared wryly that the more he saw of them the more he preferred his plantation in Sri Lanka, and he saw that she ate her portions in that lazy way of his that masked an iron will. Denise and Peter left long before they had finished their meal, much to Vinney's relief.

It was after eleven when they finally left for the drive back.

In the car, Nick said, "I'm going back to London in the morning, and I shall probably be away a week. When I return we're going to be married."

"But, Nick. . . ." Vinney began, shooting him a startled blue glance.

"But, Vinney. . . ." he mocked. "It's no use, my child, you're hooked!"

Susan said, "Denise is always with Peter Trevira these days since Nick took to going away to London. Is there anything in it?"

Her brown eyes met Vinney's blue ones innocently across the table of the farmhouse kitchen at the riding school. Motherhood suits her, thought Vinney wistfully. Her hair is a richer colour, her skin is clear and petal soft, and she has that inner glow of a happy woman lighting up the whole room. No wonder I look forward to the days I come here. The day's work was over and they were drinking tea and eating cake before Vinney left for home. At least, Susan was eating cake, a great slab of her favourite chocolate cake was fast disappearing from her plate.

"I don't know," Vinney admitted honestly. "I haven't seen much of Denise since I went to stay with Gran."

Susan licked a chunk of chocolate cream from a finger. "She won't marry him, you know," she said dramatically.

"Marry who?"

"Why, Peter Trevira, of course. He hasn't enough money for her."

Vinney stared at her wonderingly over the top of her cup.

"I thought the Treviras were wealthy landowners, and Peter is the only son."

Susan refilled her guest's cup and replenished her own. "They are and he is," laconically. "However, you may have noticed that Peter's father is still young and handsome." Her smile was dimpled. "There's no guarantee that he won't marry again and have other sons. So where does that put Peter?"

Vinney nodded and thought of her mother, an attractive, youthful-looking woman, and asked warily, "Has he anyone in mind?"

Susan shrugged. "Who knows?"

Who indeed? Vinney thought about it as she drove home to her grandmother's house in the Jag. Her horse, Prince, had been taken back to the riding school and she used the Jag since going to stay with the old lady. If her mother did marry again, what of Denise? It would certainly not suit her sister for her mother to marry into the Trevira family. Vinney liked Peter Trevira, from what little she had seen of him, and suddenly, as though in response to her thoughts, there he was dusting down his riding jacket on the roadside and there was no sign of a horse.

Vinney pulled up beside him. "Had a fall?" she asked, letting down her window.

His smile was very boyish. "Yes. Lost my horse too – my fault for riding across fields where they're putting in drains. The trouble is these days that bridle paths get fewer and fewer even on your own estates."

"Hop in. I'll give you a lift home." She leaned forward to open the door.

"Thanks." He winced as he slid into the car. "I think I've pulled a muscle." He looked round the luxurious interior as he wiped his soiled hands on his handkerchief. "Marvellous car you have. The doctor has one like it."

Vinney laughed. "I lent it to him when his was in dock."

He raised a fair brow. "That was very sporting of you. I believe you're looking after your grandmother," he went on. "How is she?"

Vinney slowed down to allow some cows the right of way. "Improving. Miss Tatton looks after her. I'm more of a companion."

Vinney drove on and Peter put his handkerchief away with a frown. "It can be a lonely world on your own," he commented. "That's why I wish Dad would marry again."

She shot him a look of surprise. "You do?"

He nodded. "Yes. It would make it easier for me to go away and leave him."

She drew a deep breath. "You're thinking of getting married?"

"No, emigrating to New Zealand. I've been thinking about it for some time."

"You have?" she queried.

For a fleeting moment their eyes met and, for fleeting seconds a disillusioned, little-boy look passed over his face like a shadow and was swiftly gone. Vinney saw the conflict in him. He obviously loved her sister, but he was not going to wait until Denise had made up her mind about him. Besides, he probably thought that he stood little chance against rivals like Nick who had so much more money than himself, and much better prospects to satisfy her.

They had reached his home and the car nosed its way along the drive. Across the spacious lawns something moved to their right among the trees.

"I think I've seen your horse," she said, and pulled up at the entrance.

Peter seemed to come out of a trance of distant thought. His eyes were dark against the paleness of his face. He had the look of a man who had lost interest in life.

"Thanks," he said, and slipped from the car to limp indoors.

The week that Nick was away in London went on wings, or so it seemed to Vinney, who was torn by the desire to see him again and feeling terrified at the prospect of sticking to her guns and refusing to marry him. She wanted him dreadfully, with a hungry yearning. Only when she was with him did the world around her make sense. The moment his lips touched hers, she felt safe and protected. Yet if she married him her life in the future would not widen into the heaven she knew was possible with him. It would, instead, gradually narrow down into the uneasy final acceptance of compromise. And all her natural instincts fought against that.

As though fitting in with her uncertainty, the weather was dismal, with grey skies bringing heavy rain. It was coming at the right time, for the farmers and the gardens accepted it gratefully, but it meant that her grandmother could not sit out in the grounds nor walk along the rose paths with herself or Miss Tatton accompanying her. So Vinney took her out for an hour in the car each day. On Thursday, the old lady was decidedly fretful and irritable, though Vinney coped pleasantly and gently with her moods.

That evening, with the old lady in bed and the house quiet and serene, Vinney, free to give way to her own depression, went wearily to her room. Her window was open and she walked towards it, breathing deeply of the air, cool and sweet, coming in from the garden below. The rain, heavy all day, had stopped leaving a freshly washed, newly minted world for the morrow. It was dark outside with no moon and the salty-tanged scent from the sea, mingling with the nocturnal perfume of the garden below had the tang of tears.

The sudden arc of light piercing the sky came from a car and eventually lowered to stab the dark grounds of the house. There was the sound of brakes on the drive. The car halted and the door slammed. Someone was calling.

Miss Tatton met her on the landing. "It's Miss Brandon, your sister. She insists on seeing you. She's in the lounge."

Denise wore a long dress and a white nylon fur jacket. Her hands were thrust in the pockets and she was pacing the carpet. Her anger came across the room in electric waves and Vinney found herself reacting in an unemotional manner. Keep cool, she told herself. You can always throw her out if she becomes too objectionable. She closed the door and Denise wheeled round.

"Yes, Denise. What do you want?"

The sea of carpet, a rich red with royal blue motifs, was

between them. Across it came the tantalizing breath of Chanel perfume.

"You're not very cordial?" The brown eyes held only an echo of her anger. "Let's say I called in for a drink and a chat."

Vinney looked at her coolly. "At this time of night? That's hardly likely. Something has upset you, and you might as well come out with it first as last. Since I haven't seen you for a while, it can hardly concern me."

"Oh, but it does." Denise loosened her jacket and sat down. "What exactly did you say to Peter the other day when you gave him a lift?"

Vinney stared at her gravely and crossed the room to stand behind a chair with her hands resting on the back of it. "How did you know I gave Peter a lift?"

Denise lifted a slim white hand and the bracelet she was wearing caught the light. The careless motion was flippant and full of meaning. The bracelet was similar to the one she herself had received from her grandmother. A present from Peter or her mother? Peter was the most likely giver, since it must have cost quite a bit, Vinney decided. She waited, repelled and contemptuous. Her face, her dark violet eyes, showed only polite attention.

"He told me." Denise leaned back in her chair and crossed her legs with the glint of silver slippers beneath the frothy skirt of her dress. Her laugh was an unpleasant tinkle. "He told me something else too. He actually thinks you're a lovely person." Her voice grated as her pleasant approach wore thin. "Oh yes, I can just imagine you putting on the charm." Her chin lifted and her lips curled. "Can I give you a lift? Dear, dear, I hope you're not hurt."

Vinney smouldered. Tense with disgust, she said bluntly, "You can cut the cackle and get down to essentials. What is it you want?"

Denise's teeth snapped. "I want to know what you said to him to persuade him to emigrate. He's going to emigrate – he told you, didn't he?"

"I don't believe he told you anything of our conversation," Vinney said with spirit. "You're just asking leading questions.

Why don't you ask Peter, since you're so eager to know?"

"But you did know about his desire to emigrate, didn't you?"

Vinney nodded. "Yes. But we had no discussion about it and your name wasn't mentioned during the short drive to his house."

"Then why is he so eager to go?" insisted Denise "It's the first I've heard about it. I dined with him that same evening and he mentioned it casually. Tonight he told me he had made definite plans to go."

Vinney did not reply for several moments but kept her eyes fixed on Denise, glamorous against the brocade of her chair in a shimmering turquoise dress, her face a hard mask, her restless fingers now toying with the bracelet on her wrist. Anyone less likely to go abroad and rough it Vinney could not imagine.

"Are you going with him?" she asked.

"Of course not. I know you would, though. You're the self-sacrificing kind, everything well lost for love. I'm not like that. What puzzles me is what caused Peter to make up his mind so soon? There are few enough presentable male escorts in this hole without being one less."

Vinney said dryly, "Maybe that's why he's going, because he knows you regard him as a convenient escort. You know he's in love with you, don't you?"

"Love!" Denise scoffed. "And how long do you think that would last, working my looks away in some benighted hole no different from this? No, thank you. I want a man with a ready-made bank balance, not one who'll have to start with a piggy bank!"

Vinney quelled a shudder as she recalled her mother's words, only the best for Denise. In spite of what Denise had done to her, she could find it in her heart to pity her. Her values of life were all wrong. One day her greedy little hands were going to take some man's heart and twist it dry of any emotion. Please God it wouldn't be Nick.

She said slowly, "It so happens that some people have more to give than others, Denise. You're not a giver, you're a taker."

"You bet I am!" harshly. "But you've some room to talk. You took Nick away from me."

Vinney's knuckles were white as she gripped the back of the chair.

"I don't know what was between you and Nick, but you know I shan't marry him. You took good care of that by filling his mind with doubts about me."

Denise looked blank. "You mean you won't marry him if he asks you?"

"He has asked me."

"He has?" Her surprise was almost comical. "And you've refused him?" The look of incredulity in the brown eyes changed slowly to one of cool calculation. Denise had been badly shaken. But she was tough. Smugly she said on breath regained, "Thanks for the information. I shall have to hang around to pick up the pieces, shan't I?" She rose languidly to her feet, and strolled casually to the door. "Oh, I almost forgot," turning slightly. "I've news for you. I've learned from Mummy that Gran has no say in the matter of a will regarding the estate. It seems Grandfather left everything in trust when he died for Daddy. Now Daddy isn't here, Mummy will be the sole beneficiary." The pink-tipped fingers slid beneath the soft collar of the white nylon fur jacket to draw it around the white column of her throat for a grand exit. "Too bad there'll be nothing for you. You'll have to make do with Aunt Phyl's legacy," was her parting shot as she swept out.

Saturday morning came with Vinney awakening from a bad dream in which she had been tossed about in a boiling sea with her father and grandmother.

Her own voice had drifted eerily across the dark waters. "Save Gran! Never mind me," she had been calling to her father when the sound of her voice had awakened her up. The house was ominously still and a strange chill feathered over her. Somehow she was prepared for the knock on her door and the shaky voice of Miss Tatton saying that the old lady had passed away in her sleep during the night.

Vinney never did remember the rest of the day. It dissolved into the mists of time with the ceaseless comings and goings that a bereavement in the family brings. The half-smile on her grandmother's still white face, as though she had found the peace for which she had been seeking, was vaguely comforting. Her going, however, had left Vinney feeling very much alone and terribly conscious of a state of vacuum in her life, for, during the last week or so, the old lady and herself had drawn very close.

It did not occur to her until the house had settled down for the night and she was on her way to bed that it was Saturday, the day when Nick was to return. How strange he had not contacted her. Too weary to conjecture, Vinney decided to forget it until the morning. But Nick did not arrive. The funeral came and went and the will was read. Apart from a bequest to Miss Tatton, an annuity from the old lady, Vinney's mother, Grace Brandon, was the only beneficiary. Old Adam Green, the gardener, had been provided for by Vinney's grandfather years ago, provided he was still in employment at the house at the time of the old lady's death.

The morning after the funeral, Vinney had breakfast and went in the Jag to see Susan at the riding school. She had the week off from duty there because Susan had insisted upon it. But then Susan had no idea how wide was the rift between her mother and Denise and herself. Since the reading of the will she had been pushed in the background by her family and the house was too quiet for her. When the old lady was there, Vinney would have welcomed the quiet house and the peace of solitude, but her mind was not at rest under the constant surveillance of her mother and the watchful reticent attitude of Denise. The atmosphere was oppressive, to say the least. She had played the piano quietly, read books and listened to the radio in between Miss Tatton bringing in coffee and biscuits. Then she had gone for long walks and returned expecting to see a letter from Nick explaining his absence, but there was no such letter, and no telephone call either. Maybe he had had more than enough of the Brandon family.

Whatever was the reason for his non-return, Vinney knew

that his present indifference could never take away the exquisite mixture of pain and joy that his love had given her. He had given her life new meaning, bringing a new depth of colour and romance into her otherwise barren existence. If he had entertained second thoughts about giving up his freedom for the more compelling demands of marriage, who was she to blame him, since she could not marry him as things stood? So what was she so unhappy about? It was in this frame of mind that Vinney decided to go to the riding school. Action was the only cure for nagging unhappy thoughts.

Her mother and Denise had arrived at the house as she was leaving. Grace Brandon, looking svelte and cool in a black cashmere sweater and black slacks relieved by a twisted golden chain around her slender throat, had favoured her with a half smile. "Going out?" she said. "Nothing for you to do now Gran's gone, is there?"

Vinney felt her throat grow tight. "No, unless you would like me to lend a hand in whatever you're doing here?"

She stood at the top of the steps leading from the front door and her mother had left the car to walk gracefully up them towards her. Denise, looking very attractive in a trouser suit in a pretty mauve colour flattering to her dark colouring, was following more leisurely.

Her mother's smile was faintly patronizing. "That won't be necessary, since Denise is here to help and we have Miss Tatton, who's staying on until everything is settled."

The easy flowing tones ate into Vinney's heart like acid. She was not wanted. Her offer of help had been flung back in her face. Gran had needed her for a while, but there was no one now who cared in the least about her. There had been a time when she had nursed her mother through her attack of 'flu that she had felt, foolishly, that the rift between them was narrowing. Now she knew with bitterness of heart that she had never been more mistaken.

Confused and shaken, her colour receding, she reacted mechanically to her mother's voice.

"If there's anything here that you would like to take away with you when you go, do tell me. I shall only be too pleased for you to have it. Oh, and by the way," Grace mentioned this as though it was ostensibly some thing which had to be included, "I've no plans for the house yet, although I've been advised to sell it."

For a long moment Vinney fought emotions threatening to choke her and an hysterical desire to escape. She managed it and put on a valiant smile, even put on a careless shrug that would have done credit to Denise.

"You must do what you feel you have to, of course. And now, if you'll excuse me, I must go."

Vinney went down the steps then to pass Denise, who had an odd expression on her face. In the Jag, she opened a window, letting the cool air blow the colour back to her cheeks. Not long ago, any suggestion of selling her grandparents' home would have shattered her. I love it, she thought, and I love Brown Thatch, but I've either outgrown them or they've outgrown me. They stifle me, harden my eyes and brain until I can't breathe. Vinney sighed and gave herself up to the pleasure of driving the Jag as the road ahead unwound before her. Thank heaven for Susan and Tim, who still made the world rosy with dreams and romance. There were many more like them, but their kind was not that numerous and she counted herself lucky to have known them.

Susan greeted her looking bright-eyed and very pretty in a pretty flowered smock. She bubbled, "You're the answer to a maiden's prayer! Be a pet and run me into the village – I've run out of knitting wool. I've cancelled all engagements at the riding school this week because you were away and it's too much for Anne to cope with on her own. I must say, though, she's coming on nicely since I took her on. So much for Tim, who said I was wrong to take a girl from school."

Vinney said soberly, "There's such a thing as being enthusiastic about the job and loving it as Anne does. I'm glad you've fixed up with someone like her, because my stay here will be short."

Susan, who had linked her arm, tossed her a startled glance on their way to the Jag.

"Must you?" she insisted. "We shall be shattered to see

you go. Surely you'll stay until I have the baby?"

Vinney shook her head. "I'm sorry, Susan, but I have to go, and soon." Her voice sounded hideously brittle and jaunty. It seemed to do so these days without her wish.

"Where are you going, may I ask?"

They were in the car now and it purred to her bidding. "I thought," said Vinney, who up to that second had thought nothing about it, "I might go away to seek the sun, Greece or somewhere like that for a while."

"Oh!" Susan seemed bereft of words and they sat in silence while the Jag ate up the distance to the village.

Now what brought that on? Vinney asked herself. Brave words – go to Greece as though her money was elastic and would stretch out indefinitely. Well, one could always get a job.

They had lunch in the village then went in the car after Susan had made several purchases for a run to the nearest town. It was an ideal day for shopping, sunny but not too hot, and they both enjoyed it immensely. But the shadow brought on by Vinney's decision to leave still hovered when they parted later that day.

Her mother and sister were leaving the house when she drove up the drive on her return. A feeling of relief washed over her to see them go, to know that their presence would not have to be suffered at dinner that evening. They were both in a good mood. It was not for her, this look of well-being, as if they had stumbled across some treasure in the house. They waited by the car while Vinney put her's in the garage.

She approached them, feeling brighter for her day out. "We always seem to be going in opposite directions," she said flippantly.

Denise raised a brow, nonplussed by the self-possession. "We've been doing it for years – or haven't you noticed?"

Her mother waved an impatient hand. Surprisingly, she said, "That was uncalled for, Denise. Have you told Vinney about the invitation to go to the Treviras' tonight?"

Denise mumbled. "No, I haven't. Peter has probably given her an invitation himself."

"How could he?" Grace Brandon exclaimed irritably, her good humour evaporating. "When it clearly stated all our names on the invitation card?" She turned to her younger daughter. "It's a farewell dinner for Peter – he's going abroad. You will come, of course."

Vinney looked her mother straight in the eye. "I'm afraid not. I hate goodbyes, especially long-drawn-out ones. I'm sure you'll make my excuse sound plausible."

"What do you think about that?" Denise's strident tones came clearly to Vinney as she entered the house. She could have laughed if it was not so painful. Carrying the war into the enemy camp was none of her choosing, but tossing brickbats back had become a kind of self-protection. Not that she would have gone to the Treviras' party. Her sensitive intuition told her that Peter Trevira was leaving home under duress. He was in love, deeply in love with Denise, and she would have hated to see her sister trampling over his feelings at a farewell party.

That evening, after dinner, Vinney put on a coat and went for a walk. The evenings were shorter now and it was not dark when her footsteps, muffled by grass, wended their way in the direction of the Treviras' house. The moon was, as yet, faint and mysterious in the darkening blue of the sky. Far below the sea washed lazily against the shore where two lovers walked, arms entwined, into the gloaming. It was a night for lovers' meeting, not for goodbyes. Sadly, her eyes sought out the big house among the trees where music wafted sweetly through open windows into the fragrance of the garden. The Treviras were popular and the party would be well attended.

She saw Peter saunter out on to the terrace . . . saw Denise join him and watched them move into the shadows. At a turn in the path with the warmth, the music and laughter to her left, Vinney paused to look back. But the trees now hid the house and the sounds grew fainter.

Vinney was on her way back in the fading light when she saw the tall figure moving with a nonchalant grace in her direction. Her face grew pale, then hot, and her heart dipped alarmingly. She breathed his name, saw the whiteness of his teeth in a smile as she hurried towards him. The next moment she was running; lovely to feel the blood rushing madly through her veins once again . . . lovely to feel life in long legs that had dragged along in another dreary lonely walk . . . to feel again the hard cheek pressed against her own, the masculine aroma of after-shave and good grooming filling her delicately moulded nostrils and . . . at last . . . his lips hard and sweet on her own. Her heart thudded into him with the laboured breathing of one who had done a four-minute mile, and when the kiss ended she reached up and framed his face with her hands to pull it down against her wet one.

"Darling," he murmured, and kissed the happy tears and the sweet fragrance of her hair. "What a welcome! It's been worth all that agonizing decision to give you more time to miss me."

"You mean you deliberately stayed away?" She lifted questioning dark blue eyes like sapphires set in the rose flush of her face. She looked radiant but puzzled. "Why?"

"This is why," he answered. His lips found hers again and they clung together closely. "God, how I've missed you," he murmured against her lips. "To think that a slender piece of nothingness could haunt my dreams and give me so many sleepless nights!" He lifted his head to look down into her face. "You are going to marry me, aren't you?"

"I love you, Nick," was all she said, but it seemed to be enough.

"You're something out of this world." His look was one of tender mocking appraisal and his eyes darkened at the gold in her hair enriched by the setting sun. "I can't wait until you're mine. I was on my way to see you, and what I wasn't going to do to you had you refused to come back with me!"

She laughed up at him joyously. "Tell me?"

"Not until I have you at my mercy beneath my own roof. And that means now."

Champagne was drunk in the cosy atmosphere of a room that was warm and inviting. They both laughed a great deal and the housekeeper was called in to join them in a toast to bride and groom, Vinney radiant with happiness, Nick disturbingly handsome and lazily amused, and the housekeeper beaming benignly on them both.

Later, they sat together on the sofa, or rather Vinney lay back against his chest as they both dreamed into the heart of a blazing log fire lighted to combat the cool of the evening. Nick picked up her hand and kissed it. Her fingers curled around his, though not possessively. For she was coming down gradually to earth after the ecstatic happiness of their reunion. For a short space of time the past had been forgotten, but now once again it was rearing its ugly head. The obstacle to their happiness was still there and Nick unwittingly brought it nearer.

"I have a special licence, my sweet. We can be married within three days. I know it follows closely on your grandmother's death, but I'm sure she would have approved," he murmured in her hair.

Vinney closed her eyes, loving his warmth at her back and the strength of purpose flowing from him. Her voice was husky with emotion. "Let's forget everything for tonight. We have each other. Don't let anything spoil it."

His deep frown met her appealing upward glance. He looked grim and determined. "We can't," he stated inexorably. "We have to thrash the whole thing out, this bogey that's bothering you. We have to talk about it. I'm happy the way things are. All I want is you. However, you aren't entirely happy and I want to know why. If it's some girlish quarrel between you and Denise, tell me about it. I know she's been bothering you in some way. . . ."

Agitatedly, Vinney broke in, "Please Nick, some other time. I can't talk to you about it now – I'm much too bemused with happiness. Oh, Nick, you don't know how I've missed you!"

Her eyes, clouded by past sorrow, met his in a kind of pathetic appeal. He regarded her intently with a dark frown for several seconds, then his mobile mouth curved into a smile and he kissed the tip of her nose.

"An armistice," he said. "Until tomorrow, on condition that you give me your word to marry me at the weekend."

Sitting in the warm circle of his arms with his deep voice vibrating through her, Vinney felt every nerve tighten inside her. It's now or never, she thought. He isn't the kind of man to be kept on tenterhooks, and that's what it amounts to. Could she make that compromise her good sense was so dead against? If not, she would lose him.

"Well?" he demanded impatiently.

"I'll marry you this weekend, you big bully. Four days? What time you think that is for a bride to get her trousseau?"

The tears spilled down her cheeks and he dealt with them gently.

"Too long for me," he murmured against her lips.

CHAPTER TEN

VINNEY awoke the following morning surprisingly early, considering how late she had gone to bed. There had been so much to arrange about the wedding which, they both agreed, was to take place at a register office in London. It had appeared that Nick had to return sooner than he had expected to Sri Lanka and they had both agreed to have a church wedding there later. Nick was picking her up at ten-thirty that morning and they were going up to London to buy whatever they needed for the wedding.

"Sure this is what you want, my sweet?" he had said. "You could have a church wedding here and be married from your own home."

But Vinney had shaken her head, knowing that her mother would want nothing to do with it. Instead of bestowing a fond mother's blessing on them both, she would receive the news in blank silence. When she did speak it would be merely to comment that she wished Vinney joy of a man whom she had stolen from her sister, and her voice would sound as if she hoped that the joy would be shortlived.

Vinney, however, was no coward, and, as she bathed and dressed, the thought occurred to her that there would be ample time for her to tell Denise what she proposed to do before Nick called for her. Having told Denise, she could enjoy her day with Nick with a sense of buoyancy and freedom to which, too long, her mind had been a stranger. Once in Sri Lanka she would put the past behind her and, with Nick's help, the pain would cease to be so acute. It would always be there in the background like an ailment to which she had become accustomed. She said nothing to Miss Tatton about her forthcoming marriage, preferring to tell Denise first so that the news would not come from another source. The task of telling her was something Vinney longed to avoid, but it had to be done, even to the final showdown and the possibility of

Denise flying into one of her rages. Her sister would have the last word, of course. It was not difficult to imagine her parting words, "Don't think you'll be happy, because you won't. Nick has heard too many home truths about you from me to ever believe you implicitly in the future."

At eight-thirty, Vinney had breakfasted all in readiness to telephone to Brown Thatch. Sandy answered to say that Mrs. Brandon was still in bed and Denise had gone down to the beach for a swim. The doctor had told her that the sea water and the exercise would be good for her knee providing she only swam in the shallows.

Ten minutes later Vinney was walking along the headland towards that part of the beach where Denise would be, the part which led down from Brown Thatch. The fragrance of trees and flowers in the full bloom of summer mingled with the scent of seaweed as she tripped lightly down a well-known path to the beach. The sun was hot on her bare arms in the blue linen dress and the sand was already warm through her sandals. The beach was deserted, and a frown touched her youthful forehead at the rough breakers rolling on the shore. Not exactly a day for bathing – it looked much too rough. As she held up her head for her face to meet the spray, her breath caught in her throat. Here was the very spot from which the tragedy had happened ten years ago. Ten years ago the treble of her clear young voice had echoed across the water. It all came back, Denise daring her to enter the water, jeering when she had done so because of that dastardly, deliberate hoax to get her there. And later Denise, callous and indifferent, swimming strongly ashore without even a backward glance to see if her young sister was going to make it back again after an all-out effort to swim out to her. Vinney had not come down to bathe again since her return home because she wanted to forget. Now, as she stood again in the place where it all happened, the past came back to her as clear as though it had happened yesterday. If I close my eyes, was her thought, I could open them and swear to seeing Denise in the water.

Where was she? Not on the shore. Her eyes concentrated on the heaving mass of sea. Not far out the waves washed around a tiny island which the full tide covered completely and around which strong undercurrents were a snare for unwary swimmers. As children, they had always given it a wide berth when bathing. What appeared to be a bit of driftwood was much further out, and Vinney quelled a shiver. It couldn't possibly be Denise that far out. She was a strong swimmer, but surely she would not defy doctor's orders, not with an injured knee-cap. With a hand shielding her eyes from the glare of the sun, Vinney tried to identify the floating object. Then she saw two arms cleaving through the water as though endeavouring to make headway to the shore. The next moment they were flung high into the air and there was nothing there.

When it appeared again a cry came and was lost in the noise of the sea. It occurred to her that whoever it was could be in difficulties, and that it might not be Denise. Vinney remembered that last time when her sister had lured her out on the pretext of drowning. Was she doing the same thing again – this time with a more sinister motive? An arm went up again, again the cry for help. Vinney hesitated no longer. Unzipping her dress, she struck out in the water, clad only in her bra and panties, to swim with grim determination.

Unlike ten years ago, Vinney was no puny swimmer. Even so, swimming against the tide in anything but calm sea was giving her a beating. The waves buffeted her about as she cut her way steadily through them, knowing that whoever was out there would not survive unless they were reached in time. It seemed to take hours to battle to the spot and, at last, making a final spurt, she looked around and saw nothing. Then something bobbed up on the water, her heart lurched at the sight of the grey, unconscious face . . . of Denise. No trick this time. With maniacal strength, Vinney gripped her firmly, turned towards the shore and wished with all her heart that it was not so far away. That final spurt had taxed her strength and Denise, now a dead weight, had the look of one who had gone past human aid. Fiercely, Vinney refused to accept it, and struck out gallantly. The sun still shone overhead and she blessed the tide going in their direction. The return journey was even more agonizingly slow, with the ominously still body of Denise trailing grey-faced in the water with her. It was not too late to save her. It just could not be. When they reached the shore Denise would come round with artificial respiration. Speed was the most important thing . . . speed . . . speed. The word beat in Vinney's brain, until her breath began to draw in between agonizing gulps.

Would she make it? Any minute now her limbs would refuse to go any further and her heart seemed to be thumping a hole in her ribs. The pain at the back of her neck increased and her receding consciousness was halted by a cry. Someone was coming, someone who sounded like Nick . . . Oh, the blessed touch of helping hands . . . "Can you make it, darling? Just tread water and you're there," Nick was saying.

Painfully, her breath coming in agonizing spasms, Vinney relinquished her burden. "Yes . . . yes . . . hurry . . . Denise is in . . . a bad . . . way."

With leaden limbs, Vinney struck out for the shore to stumble eventually through the shallows in the wake of Nick, who had turned anxiously to see if she was all right before carrying his burden up the beach. Gallantly, she lifted a hand accompanied by a weak smile to reassure him. Then she followed. Denise's arms were swinging slackly and water was trickling from her mouth as Nick placed her face down on the sand to begin working grimly on her back. The silence was terrifying and eerie and the fact that Nick was not speaking meant that he was going all out to force life back into that quiet, inert figure.

Vinney had dropped to her knees a few feet away. Her eyes were riveted on them. Nick was sweating and a lock of hair fell across his brow. He had obviously flung off his jacket, for his shirt and slacks were plastered to his long, lean form. The silence seemed now to stretch to eternity. She closed her eyes and her fevered mind feared the worst. Then she remembered no more.

"Come on, my sweet, open your mouth!"

The deep voice reached down into her subconsciousness and her eyes opened. She was sitting up on the sand in the curve of Nick's arm and her head lay against his shoulder. Obediently

Vinney opened her mouth and a little brandy from the flask in his hand trickled down her throat. It made her cough.

"Another sip, to please me," he insisted tilting the flask.

The raw spirit ran through her veins like fire. Recent events, though still cloudy, were again taking shape in her mind. The tears gathered in her eyes and a hand weakly pushed the brandy flask away. Her face turned into his chest and she began, involuntarily, to weep.

"We were too late, weren't we?" she sobbed.

His hand cupped the back of her head, moving round it soothingly as he bent his head to kiss her hair.

"No. And where do you get the 'we' from?" Nick demanded. "You saved her."

A sob caught in her throat and she lifted her head to brush the tears fiercely from her eyes. "You . . . you mean Denise is alive?" she asked weakly.

"Yes. She's back there wrapped in my jacket with the coast-guard. He arrived in his little runabout, having seen us from the lookout post. And that's where we're going. He's taking us back to Brown Thatch."

Nick stuffed the brandy flask into the pocket of his slacks and scooped her up into his arms as he spoke, and Vinney nestled against him with a prayer of gratitude.

At Brown Thatch blankets and hot water bottles had been the order of the day. Sandy had insisted that the former were better than electric blankets for the moment. Nick had gone home and changed and now he was sitting in the lounge at Brown Thatch drinking coffee with Vinney, clad in her crumpled blue linen brought up from where she had cast it on the shore.

"What about our shopping expedition . . .?" Nick was saying when her mother came in.

"Denise would like to see you, Nick," she said in a strained voice. "The doctor has just gone."

"How is she?" Vinney asked, moving from the warm circle of Nick's arm to put down her coffee cup.

"She's going to be all right."

"That's good." Nick's hand sought Vinney's and his fingers curled around hers. "Come on, my sweet, we'll go up together." He rose to his feet and pulled her up with him.

"I'd like to speak to Vinney, Nick. I won't keep her long. Do go up and see Denise."

Her mother's cool tones struck a shiver of apprehension through Vinney's slim frame as Nick hesitated, seemed about to say something, then changed his mind and left the room.

"Sit down, Vinney."

Grace Brandon's expression was reflective and, as her daughter sat down, she walked over to the window to present her slim back to her. The room, filled with summer sun, held a strange chill for Vinney, who felt the shadow of something hurtful enclosing her. For an instant neither of them spoke. Her mother stood there looking through the window. Retaining that position, she began to speak.

"I don't know the facts of what happened out there on the beach this morning. But from what I can gather from Denise, Nick saved her life. All I know is that Nick carried Denise up to her room and told me to send for the doctor. I suppose her knee let her down when she was in the water."

At this juncture, Grace turned slowly to face her incredulous daughter calmly after making this most surprising statement. Then she went on,

"I can be very ruthless where Denise's happiness is concerned. She lost her father through no fault of her own and I've striven to make up for it. I've decided to sell everything here and take a flat in London where I can mix with old friends from the theatre and maybe get a job acting again. But first I want to see Denise settle down and get married. How far has this affair of yours with Nick gone?"

Vinney looked for a moment as if she had been shocked out of her senses. Her colour changed from blush rose to white and she trembled inwardly. There was a rushing sound in her ears and pain laid deep shadows in her dark, blue eyes. No one was less capable of speech in that moment.

Her mother went on, "I use the word affair because I'm sure that's all there is between you. Denise wears Nick's ring and, much as I dislike saying this, he could have taken you on the rebound after quarrelling with her. She's never told me what happened between them to account for his cooling off, so I can only assume that it was some silly little squabble which could have been put right had you not come along." Her voice hardened. "I never wanted you to come back – I knew you would bring only trouble. I'm asking you to go away now, this minute, and give Denise her chance of happiness with Nick. With you gone, I'm sure he'll turn to her."

Vinney had the urge to put up an arm to ward off further attack. Her mother's attitude was more than sinister towards her; it was like facing a furnace that one had to step back from or be burned. The sunlight streamed across the room to spray gold dust into her hair and the colour hastening back to her pale face gave her a very young, vulnerable look.

Slowly she rose to her feet and her youthful dignity sat well on her slender shoulders. Her voice was perfectly calm.

"You'll never know what happened this morning from me . . ." Her teeth steadied her lower lip, but it was no use. The word, "Mummy," would not come out. She tried again. "It seems you and Denise have everything planned. I wish you luck. I'm leaving here, and this minute. I have only one thing to say – I hope you meet with more kindness from your theatre friends than you've shown to me, your daughter. Goodbye!"

Rushing blindly from the house, Vinney never stopped running until she arrived back at Four Cedars, her grandmother's house. It was only as she entered her room that her brain relaxed into a semblance of calm. Like a mechanical doll she packed her cases and ran out to her car, past the astonished face of Miss Tatton.

Vinney drove at a speed to escape, as it were, from her own misery. Her mind now was ice cool, her hands steady on the car wheel, taking the bends with one swoop. There was a rewarding slickness in the way the Jag responded to her demands. Taking the hump-backed bridge in the village faster than common sense demanded, she wrenched the car around the corner and sailed on regardless.

The miles slipped beneath the car bonnet and soon the inn where Nick had taken her to dine flashed by – enchanted place, enchanted hours. But she must not think of Nick whose deep voice, caressive touch and deceptively lazy way of moving, sent the blood pounding through her veins. The greatest tragedy of life was the mistakes one made. One of her mistakes had been to return home and hope for mercy from a mother who had no idea of the meaning of the word. But her return home had made her sadder and wiser. One thing she had learned from the whole miserable business was that it did not matter in the least now whether her mother learned the truth about the part Denise had played in the tragedy of her father's death or not. It didn't matter any more. What did matter was the love she felt for Nick, a love so real, so deep, that everything else faded into insignificance beside it. Entirely absorbed in her own reasons for returning home, she had not seen that her need of him was far greater than the need for her family. And she had left him to Denise.

Nick had taken the stairs up to Denise's room two at a time. She was in bed, wearing the fondant pink bedjacket trimmed with white swansdown; her eyes and thick rope of hair over one shoulder took on a richer brown. She looked exhausted but pretty as she lowered her thick eyelashes effectively against the pallor of her face as he strode across the room to greet her.

One hand was proffered languidly for him to take. Her voice was honey-sweet. "Hello, Nick. I had to see you, to thank you for saving my life."

Holding her hand, he lowered himself down on to the bed to face her, and gave a wry smile. "I didn't save you. Vinney did," he corrected her gravely.

Her fingers curled possessively around his. "My dear Nick, don't be so modest! It's just like you to want someone else to take the credit." She was vastly amused. "Why, Vinney couldn't save herself, let alone me. Do you know that she once plunged into the sea thinking that I was in difficulties and almost lost her own life in the process?"

168

Nick leaned forward intently. "Did she now? This is most interesting. Tell me more." His eyes narrowed at the hard mockery on her face as she watched him covertly. "When did this happen?" he insisted when no answer was forthcoming. "I suppose it was years ago."

His smile, the deceptive lightness of his voice deceived her as to the real reason of his probing as he had meant it to do.

Denise lowered her eyelashes to hide the malevolent gleam in her eyes.

"Oh yes," carelessly, "it happened years ago. Poor Vinney was hopeless at school sports. I was the one who took all the prizes."

Her attempt at modesty, the creamy sweetness of her voice was meant to impress. Nick raised a quizzical brow. He was not impressed.

"But she did try to save your life." He leaned nearer and murmured, "Don't you think it was very brave of a little girl to go to the rescue of her big sister at the risk of her own life?"

So she's told him, thought Denise vindictively. The little bitch! She won't get away with it – I'll see to that.

"I don't know what she's told you," she said, "but it's just like her to make herself out to be a heroine. Vinney's the romantic type who believes in dreams."

Nick bunched his fist and made a playful feint beneath her chin.

"This is no dream. Vinney is a heroine. She saved your life this morning almost at the expense of her own. I don't know how she did it in such a rough sea. Poor sweet, she was all in when she handed your unconscious body to me a few strokes from the shore."

Denise recoiled. Two vivid spots of colour stood out in the paleness of her face. Hatred of her sister was like poison in her mouth. The endearment he had used could only mean that she had lost him irrevocably to Vinney. It did not help to see that he had gone pale at the memory of that morning – that a firm brown hand was raking through the crisp dark hair at the thought of it.

"God," he was saying, "I must have aged ten years when

I had to leave Vinney in the water in order to bring you ashore."

Denise was shaking her head, refusing to believe that Vinney had saved her life. She moistened dry lips. "But I was unconscious. It was you who squeezed the water from my lungs, you who saved me. Vinney couldn't have done it," she insisted.

"You don't know your own sister." Nick was smiling tenderly at some secret thought. "She's quite a girl. She would have saved you had I not been there, artificial respiration, the lot. Vinney's a girl who never gives up."

His praise produced startling results. Denise seemed to shrink before his eyes. Her nostrils thinned, her face was a deadly white mask and her eyes blazed malevolently. Never gives up, was what he had said. She moved against her pillows uneasily, wanting to strike his dark sardonic face. But all she could do was to stare at him fascinated and repelled as he rose indolently to his feet to push his hands into his pockets. He knew. He knew all about the part she had played ten years ago – that she had put all the blame for the tragedy on Vinney. His next words proved this was so.

Narrow-eyed and intent, he drawled slowly, "You said something about Vinney attempting to rescue you before almost at the cost of her own life. On that occasion . . . did it end in tragedy for someone else?"

Denise drew a rasping breath as if he had struck her across the face. Her lips were colourless and hardly moved. "She's told you, hasn't she? Told you that I played a joke on her in order to get her into the water?" Her voice became an unpleasant snarl. "Well, it's all lies . . . only her word against mine. Naturally, she . . . would deny being the cause of Daddy losing his life."

She was becoming agitated and Nick lifted a hand. "Look, I'm sorry to upset you. The interrogation is over. I've proved my point." His mouth thinned contemptuously. "As it happens, Vinney told me nothing about your part in the affair. You did. If you remember, you told me just now that Vinney almost lost her life in an attempt to rescue you. As I could hardly imagine her doing it more than once before today, I rightly assumed that the only other time was on the day her father died. It's obvious to me that you found it easy to put the blame on someone who was too ill at the time to defend herself."

The silence in the room was broken only by the rasping fury of Denise's deep breathing. "Try to prove it, that's all. Now get out!" she hissed, and shuddered at the closing of the door.

Grace Brandon was alone in the lounge when he entered to look around in search of Vinney.

"Where's Vinney?" he demanded curtly.

Shaken out of her usual calm, Grace gave him a startled upward glance and returned the coffee she had been drinking to the low table beside her chair. A slight frown creased her usually smooth forehead.

"I understood she had gone to join you in Denise's room," she answered. "Is anything wrong? You look angry. It isn't Denise, is it?" An anxious note deepened her voice. "She's all right, isn't she?"

"Apart from feeling a little sorry for herself, Denise is all right," impatiently. "It's Vinney that I'm concerned about. Where is she?"

A faint shrug from the elegant shoulders told him that this cold statue of a woman did not share his concern for her younger daughter – never had.

"If Vinney hasn't joined you then she must have returned to Four Cedars." Grace's tone was one to coax him to be reasonable. A degree of warmth flickered in her eyes. "Sandy will be in presently with fresh coffee, and we can ask her where Vinney is. Do sit down. I haven't thanked you yet for saving my daughter's life. I'm very grateful, Nick."

His mouth thinned and he did not sit down. "You seem to be labouring under a misapprehension, Mrs. Brandon. I didn't save your daughter's life, Vinney did."

If Grace had looked startled before, she was now absolutely flabbergasted. "Are you sure?" she gasped.

He raised a quizzical brow. "She didn't tell you when you asked her to stay behind just now?"

Grace was confused but wary. "No . . . I mean, I didn't know. From what Denise told me, it was you who brought her round and wrapped her in the jacket you'd flung off before entering the water."

"Do you always believe what Denise tells you?" Nick waved a hand angrily. "You have two daughters, Mrs. Brandon, not one. You happened to believe the wrong one as you did ten years ago."

Grace drew herself up haughtily. "I haven't the least idea what you're talking about."

Nick lowered himself on to the arm of an easy chair. His smile was sardonic. "Stick around and you'll soon know. It never occurred to you, did it, that Denise was the prime cause of you losing your husband, not Vinney, ten years ago?"

"Look, what is this?"

Nick surveyed her contemptuous look with a degree of calm. "It's perfectly true. I had the information from Denise just now – given under duress, but undisputedly the truth, which she will deny to you with her last breath."

"If you've been upsetting her . . ." Grace rose to her feet and Nick motioned her to resume her seat.

"Sit down," he commanded. "You'll find it interesting. That's better." This as she obeyed. "I could be wrong, but isn't Denise the one who's been upsetting everyone for quite a long time? Even you, occasionally, judging by that glimpse I had once of her fiendish temper."

"I don't know where all this is supposed to be leading. but I hope you are aware that Denise will never be nearer death than she was on your own admission this morning. As for Vinney saving her. . . ." Grace Brandon's lip curled.

Nick looked fit to do murder. His voice was rapier-sharp and his eyes narrowed cruelly on her withdrawn expression. "Vinney deserves a medal for gallantry. God knows how she did it. I arrived on the scene just as she was about to struggle from the water with an unconscious Denise. Yes, unconscious,

Mrs. Brandon, with Vinney at the end of her tether."

Enlightenment slowly dawned in her eyes. "Of course, I can see what happened. Denise's knee let her down, which was why the doctor told her to swim in shallow water. I fail to see why Vinney was so exhausted bringing her in."

Sardonically, Nick said, "You only see what you want to see, don't you, Mrs. Brandon? Denise is a headstrong, wilful girl who's gone through life doing exactly as she pleases, and that meant disobeying any order for her own good. It so happens that on this occasion she swam out into deep water against orders, exactly as she did ten years ago when her father was drowned. Vinney went out to rescue her then as she did this morning, only ten years ago Denise had flouted your wishes and pretended to be drowning in order to get her sister into the water. Then she swam ashore and callously abandoned her young sister to make her way back in an exhausted state. That's when your husband came into the picture. The coast-guard saw it all."

Grace looked stricken. "I remember now. His wife was having a baby and she was critically ill for four days, which was why he wasn't there to give evidence at the inquest. He was miles away in the hospital with her. He must have been on his way there with her and told no one what he'd seen. I sent Vinney away," she said tonelessly. "And I've sent her away again."

Nick went tense. "What did you say to her when I left you together?" he demanded. The gleam in his eyes was one of goaded fury.

Grace retreated perceptively, said weakly, "I'm sorry. I'm not sure." A hand went to her throat. "One thing I must know. Denise still wears your ring. How are things between you?"

Nick had risen to his feet, impatient of the delay, to wave a deprecating hand. "It isn't my ring," he vouchsafed coldly and clearly. "I bought it for Denise when she was in Sri Lanka. She admired it, couldn't afford it, so I bought it for her as a present. It was never remotely connected with an engagement ring."

"But she wore it on her engagement finger?"

He shrugged wide shoulders. "It was the only finger it would fit comfortably, so she said. Mrs. Brandon," he went on, "I'm not concerned with Denise. Vinney is the girl I love. I'm going to marry her with or without your blessing. Now where is she?"

Grace looked blank. "I . . . I don't know. Possibly at Four Cedars packing her cases." She sighed. "I suppose it's no use saying how sorry I am?"

Nick had already taken a pace or two away from her. Now he paused, his face grim. "You don't have to say that to me, Mrs. Brandon. Vinney is the one you should say it to. I only know one thing." His mouth thinned and he went pale beneath his tan. "If I lose Vinney the light will have gone out of my life and nothing will ever be the same again."

He strode to the door and stepped aside for Sandy to enter with a tray of fresh coffee. Sandy was not in the best of tempers. What with the extra running about that morning, the hot water bottles, the doctor calling and the daily woman not turning up to help with the chores, she had been knocked completely off her stride. But when she saw Nick, her worries about a late lunch were completely charmed away. In her opinion this delightful young man, who had been blessed with more than his share of charm and good looks, plus an enchanting voice that could made even her old knees feel weak, was a delight to wait upon.

With a smile, Sandy carried in the tray and turned as the door closed behind Nick.

"He's gone!" she exclaimed on a disappointed echo, to find she was talking to thin air.

Grace had rushed across the room to the front entrance in time to see him sliding into his car on the drive.

"Please do something for me, Nick," she called. "Tell Vinney I'm sorry for everything."

He gave her an ironic glance before he thrust the car forward to shoot along the drive at speed. Then he had gone.

CHAPTER ELEVEN

VINNEY had driven solidly for two hours, passing hamlets and woods gay with their summer raiment, but the beauty of it all only registered vaguely on her disturbed mind. She was at the stage when nothing seemed real. It was all like some horrible dream that did not make sense. In Malta, she had thought of her home at Brown Thatch with all the longing of an exile. Once she was there, her wish had been never to leave it, as though nothing in the world existed but her home by the sea with all the memories of youth. This last final break with it had stripped the future of any reason for existing.

There had been times in Malta when the enchantment of her life there had been coloured by the fact that some day the dream of being reconciled with her family would really come true. It was only too clear now that it had never been any more than a dream, a dream that only a romantic idiot like herself would believe in. Aunt Phyllis had been a romantic too, and she had never changed, never grown bitter because her own mother had cast her out. If at times her aunt had appeared wistful when she recalled some incident in her childhood, her expression, her memories of her mother and her home had always been tender and sweet. And that's how I shall always be, Vinney thought. I can never change even if I wanted to. In a way it was a relief not having to camouflage her feelings any more . . . to smile and act naturally in the strained atmosphere surrounding her at Brown Thatch . . . not to show her hurt at some caustic witty remark from Denise . . . and to bear without flinching the total indifference of her mother.

Aunt Phyllis's maxim had been that there was always some good to be gleaned from any catastrophe, however great. Thinking on this, Vinney recapped and gleaned the good things from her disastrous return home . . . her reunion with her old school friend, Susan, the opportunity to make her grandmother's last days happy ones, helping to save Denise's life . . . and last but not least, Nick. A hollow feeling of lone-liness and need lay heavily on her heart, transmitting itself to her stomach. The disgruntled rumblings in that region were reminding her that it had missed lunch and that the hollow feeling would become less painful when she had something to eat. Not that she was feeling in the least hungry. But as the Jaguar would also need refuelling, it would be a good idea to drive on to the next filling station and restaurant.

The filling station and restaurant adjoined and were set in gardens bright with trees, shrubs and flowers. Vinney drove into the restaurant car park, deciding to eat first before having the car filled. A clock struck four as she entered a beautifully carpeted foyer leading into a dining room of small, immaculate tables each containing a menu card in the shape of a smiling chef.

Upon request, a pot of tea, home-made scones, jam and fresh cream were brought by a pretty young waitress. The tea service was silver, the cup, saucer and dishes were eggshell blue china, incentives to the poorest appetite. Vinney managed two scones and two cups of delicious tea. By the time she left the restaurant her world did not seem so grey.

She had drawn in at the filling station and the attendant was checking the Jag's intake when the car roared by, pulled up sharply along the road ahead hidden by trees and reversed to the shrieking of breaks to return and slide in behind her. She saw the attendant, a good-looking young man with his uniform hat set at an angle, hang up the nozzle to a pump, give an exaggerated cringe at the shrieking of brakes, then stroll to her car window for her to pay him.

His twinkling eyes had ranged appraisingly over the red Jag, now they did the same over Vinney.

"Super car. Super girl," he murmured, taking the money. "And, in case you don't know it," accompanied by a sideways jerk of the head to the car behind her, "James Bond has just arrived to complete the set-up!"

Vinney smiled as he touched his cap, put her purse in the glove compartment and ignored the commotion going on behind. Masculine voices, the slam of a car door from behind were also ignored as she started the Jag. The next moment the window on her left was blacked out and a head appeared.

Nick said peremptorilly, "Keys to the boot, please, then move up. I'll drive."

Bewildered and mesmerized, Vinney handed over the keys and shivered, for his anger was almost tangible. Then she sat motionless while he presumably put his own cases in the boot of her car. Miserably she remembered that today they were to have gone to London to do some shopping for . . . for their wedding on Saturday. Mechanically, her slim form slid along into the next seat and, after a hasty consultation with the attendant, Nick was sliding in beside her. He was pushing his wallet into his pocket and reaching grimly for the controls, his profile clear-cut and set in no mood for conversation.

The Jaguar responded to his touch and roared away with frightening speed. The silence was interminable while a chorus of little voices sang inside Vinney. Nick was here beside her, tense with anger but here just the same. He had come after her and brought his cases too. She was to have a second chance. Her lower lip trembled and she bit on it hard, but she could not prevent the sob that started from deep inside her from reaching her lips. With her face buried in her hands, she was weeping quietly.

Nick spoke at last. "Why did you do it?" He tossed her a glance and continued, narrow-eyed and unsmiling, "Didn't you know what you were doing to me?"

Vinney shook her head, groped in her bag for her handkerchief and mopped at her eyes.

She mumbled, knowing it sounded inadequate, "I'm sorry."

His voice was on ice. He pulled the car viciously round a bend. "What for? For showing me, rather callously, that you don't want to marry me?"

"No, no and no!" she cried. "That isn't true. I love you and . . . I want to marry you. How can you think that?"

Irritably, he demanded, "What else could I think with you running out on me like that? Was it something your mother said to you when I went upstairs?"

Vinney dried her eyes and leaned back in her seat. The sobs

still shook her inwardly and each indrawn breath was like a sword thrust.

She looked down at the drenched ball of her handkerchief, and said miserably, "I did what I thought was best for all of us. Mother only spoke the truth when she said that it would be far better for all concerned if I went away . . . I was wrong to come home again, I see that now." His sudden indrawn breath made her rush on. "By that I don't mean I'm sorry I met you. I . . . I could have returned home and bought a little place of my own instead of bothering . . . the family. That way I wouldn't have barged in between what was between you and Denise."

He said in a strange voice, "Are you sorry for falling in love with me?"

"Oh dear, I'm not putting this very well, am I? It isn't like that at all. I love you more than my life, yet somehow I haven't felt free to love you. I've even doubted your love for me."

"Charming! Is that why you ran away?"

Her restless hands were pulling at the handkerchief. "I . . . I think it was the culmination of events that made me do that. I . . . felt that I couldn't take any more."

"Why didn't you tell your mother that you'd saved Denise's life?" he asked her bluntly.

Her eyes widened on his profile to their full extent. "I didn't save her. You did. You carried her ashore and brought her round."

He agreed. "After you'd trailed her body half way across the ocean. My dear girl, if you hadn't gone to her rescue when you did she would never have survived. You saved her life all right and she wasn't able to use any kidology, as on that last occasion which ended in tragedy. I'm alluding to the last time you plunged in the sea in an effort to save your worthy sister ten years ago," he finished.

They were nearing the outskirts of London and he swung the car suddenly into a cul-de-sac forming the entrance to a park. Switching off the engine, he put an arm on the wheel and turned round to face her. He was smiling.

By this time Vinney had recovered her breath. She whispered, "You mean, you know about last time . . . when Daddy died?"

He nodded. "Yes, from Denise. It was hardly a confession on her part. Let's say it slipped out. Sufficient to say that I know what's been bothering you. I told your mother how she had misjudged you through the years. I also told her that you had saved her precious daughter."

Vinney had lost her breath again. She was trembling now and he made no move to touch her.

"You did?" she gasped.

Again he nodded. "Those few moments with your mother were most revealing. Through my summary of her, I began to know the real you . . . that lonely child who had been starved of affection and who had suffered an adolescence tortured by the thought of being unjustly blamed for her father's death." He framed her face gently in his hands. "My poor darling, and you couldn't tell me about it because of putting the blame on someone you thought I loved."

His lips closed on her trembling ones and his gentleness changed to a demanding elation that scared her even while the fire of it ran through her veins like mercury. Against the sweet answering pressure of her lips he murmured, "Happy now?"

"Yes."

"That was the bogey between us, wasn't it?"

"Yes."

"And there's nothing else worrying you?"

"No."

"Love me?" His lips moved down to her neck.

"You know I do!" she smiled.

"Show me." He laughed as she quivered in his ever-tightening hold. He was an ardent lover now, his tanned cheek moving over hers caressingly. He breathed in the fragrance of her hair as he crushed her slim suppleness against him. And as her arms crept up around his neck, his mouth sought to imprison hers again. It seemed to Vinney that those soul-shattering kisses set the seal of happiness on her life ahead. She clung, discovering her love to be as insatiable as his.

When she was quivering and spent he released her to gaze ardently at her mouth, beautiful from his kisses. Her eyes were no longer bewildered and unhappy. They were deep blue pools of loveliness in which he would willingly drown. His eyes darkened and he looked down at her with all the passion and desire of a man who knows he has met his true mate. He devoured the gold of her hair, her eyes luminous with happiness, the soft red mouth and the tender sweep of her jaw.

"I love everything about you," he whispered. "I love the gold of your hair, the curly tendrils against the blush of your cheeks, your blue eyes innoc.... of guile . . . the way you walk, your slender charm, the quiet musical pitch of your voice . . . the way you say 'Oh dear' and the fact that you're so delicious to kiss. I can't wait for that first morning when I'll wake to find you there beside me, knowing that we're going to spend the rest of our lives together."

He said much more, and Vinney felt the blood pounding through her veins just to have him there speaking the nonsense all lovers like to hear. He was grinning now.

"I could sit here for hours telling you why I love you. Some of the reasons could surprise you . . . some could even embarrass you, so I'll tell you more when I can't scare you away . . . when we're married." He broke off to consult his wrist watch. "We'd better be making tracks for London. We'll put up at a hotel for the night and do our shopping tomorrow."

Nick had booked two sets of rooms with his on the floor above her own. He had ordered dinner for two to be sent up to his rooms where they had dined together in a deep-carpeted, graciously decorated and furnished room attended by a waiter who seemed delighted to be waiting upon such a charming young couple. Over dinner they had laughed a lot and toasted each other in champagne and had their coffee later seated together on the sofa. Resting back against Nick, Vinney revelled in the comforting warmth of strong, protective arms.

"Hmm, this is lovely," was her contented comment before

she alighted from her pink cloud to dwell upon mundane things. With her own spacious hotel room with an adjoining private bathroom in mind, she added, "Our rooms here are going to cost the earth."

Nick kissed the top of her hair. "So what?"

She looked up at him with serious blue eyes. "I insist upon paying my share, that's all. We're not married yet – and, while we're on the subject of marriage, I'm not the heiress Denise has made me out to be. . . ."

Nick cut in lazily, "Darling, what is this? You know I'm a wealthy man."

"I know. But I'm not a wealthy woman, Nick. I've told no one this, but I gave the villa Aunt Phyllis left to me in Malta to Bruno, her favourite nephew. He loved it and, as he was a bit of a playboy, I wanted to give him an incentive to marry and settle down, to . . . to make something of himself. You understand?" Her eyes appealed him to. "The estate consisted partly of small dwellings on the island occupied by Uncle Paul's relatives, which I made over to them. The rest, which included Aunt Phyllis's personal belongings, I kept."

For long moments his dark eyes looked deeply into hers. Then gradually his mobile mouth curved into a tender smile and he brought his lean hard cheek down to her soft one.

"All this is irrelevant, my sweet," he whispered in her ear. "I shall foot the bill here or there'll be trouble. Is that understood? As far as what you've just told me is concerned, it only goes to show what a really sweet, unselfish person you are, entirely opposite to what Denise implied with her lies."

A tremor went through her as she recalled the decision she had made not to marry him until it was possible to refute everything Denise had accused her of.

"So you did take notice of what she said about me!"

Her voice was so piteous that he acted upon it immediately. "Hey now! Just a minute." He lifted his head and looked down sternly into her face. "Of course I took notice of what she said about you. Anything anyone has to say about you interests me, since I not only intend to be your lover and husband, but also your protector and friend. Now kiss me before I beat you.'

He was laughing as he made the teasing threat, and Vinney was only too happy to oblige as he bent his head.

CHAPTER TWELVE

THE next day began with breakfast together in the hotel dining room, then a morning spent around the shops in the enchanting heart of the city. They had lunch back at the hotel, smooth home-cooked paté with crisp rolls, a fine coq au vin with mixed vegetables and a superb iced soufflé made with Grand Marnier. The coffee and a litre of Bordeaux finished off an excellent meal. In the afternoon they went down the Thames and had tea on board the boat. It was a day Vinney knew she would remember and cherish all her life.

"Would you like to be married in the village church at Downsend?" Nick asked when they were drifting back along the Thames later that afternoon. "It could be arranged with little trouble."

Vinney digested this, then shook her head. "No, your way is much better. We'll go to the register office as planned, then be married in Sri Lanka in church. Denise, I'm sure, wouldn't come to the wedding, neither would Mummy if we married back home. Besides, I've no wish to embarrass them further, but I would like Susan and Tim to come to our wedding."

"Exactly my sentiments," Nick agreed. "I can see we're going to be wonderfully happy together. What do you say to us staying at the hotel until we're married and also spending the first night of our honeymoon there before going on to Paris?"

Her eyes shone up at him. "Oh yes, let's!" she breathed ecstatically.

On her wedding morning, Vinney breakfasted in her room. The wedding wasn't until three o'clock that afternoon and Nick had left early to drive in the Jaguar to Downsend to settle everything there. He planned to leave his housekeeper in charge. "Even if we do decide to live abroad," he had said to Vinney the previous evening, "our sons will no doubt be

183

educated here, so what better than a house for them to live in while they're here?" He had laughed at her blushes. "You do want children?"

"Of course."

Vinney was thinking about it as she lay in her perfumed bath. It was all too wonderful to bear thinking about. Susan and Tim were having lunch with her at the hotel and Tim was to be best man.

The wedding had gone without a hitch. Susan and Tim had arrived, Susan trim and becoming in a dress and coat cunningly contrived to hide her condition. In the register office Vinney and Susan had transformed the unromantic interior with their grace, beauty and obvious happiness. In an outfit of sapphire blue and white, the bride had looked ravishing and had turned many heads beside Nick's when leaving the register office in brilliant sunshine.

Nick had booked a private room at the hotel for the reception and it was here that the telegrams of congratulations arrived, including one from Grace and Denise. Vinney suspected that Nick had let it be known where the reception was to be held when he had gone down to Downsend that morning. It was all part of the perfect arrangements he had made to give her ultimate happiness on the most important day of her life. Denise, she learned, had gone back to modelling and had accepted an assignment in America, since her mother's flat, when Grace moved to London, would be sure to have a spare room in it for her to return to.

The reception was over. The guests had left for home when Nick suggested a late night show to finish off their day. But for Vinney, it was enough to take a stroll in the light summer evening, to look, to listen, and to absorb her husband who, from now on, would always walk beside her. In the fading light of a summer sky, a sliver of a new moon waited for the sun to take its final bow and the lights of their hotel came on as they walked up the steps hand in hand as though to welcome them.

"I love you," murmured Nick, taking her in his arms after closing the door of their room to shut out the world. "You're the most wonderful thing that's ever happened to me. I know we're going to be very happy together." He looked deep into her luminous eyes and the blood pounded in her heart. "Mind you, you took a lot of convincing and ran away like a scared rabbit. Scared now?"

He raised a tantalizing brow and her face coloured like a rose. "Not at all," said she demurely. "Should I be?"

"Most certainly you should after my threat of what I would do to you if you did run away from me," was the cool answer, denying the deepening gleam of amusement in his eyes. "It never occurred to you, did it, to tell me what was bothering you and to ask for my help? I could have sorted things out much quicker between you and your family if you had trusted me," soberly. "Saved you heartache too."

The shadow of the past clouded her eyes. "Why should I expect you to take the word of a stranger against that of Denise whom you already knew?"

"Because, my sweet, I loved you from the moment I saw you." He gave her a gentle shake, said darkly, "You're not convinced even now, are you?"

Vinney raised her hands to clasp them around his neck. "Convince me," she murmured provocatively.

He smiled, kissed her lingeringly, then let her go.

"I don't intend to convince you here when I can do so much better in bed." He quirked a disparaging glance in that direction. "While it isn't exactly a single bed, it isn't a marriage bed either."

"We'll make it one," she told him.

The room was filling with shadows when Vinney climbed into bed. Nick had wanted to book a bridal suite for their wedding night, but Vinney, who loved this room because it was impregnated with Nick's presence, had urged him to keep it. He would not always give in to her – he was too much a man. But Vinney did not want it any other way. He would make an exciting lover and husband. Looking back, her decision to return home had been the right one after all. It had brought a better understanding of her mother's attitude towards her, believing as she had that her youngest child had been responsible for the two tragedies in her life, losing her chance of fame on the stage and losing her husband. Now, with the help of Gran's money, she could go to London and try again for stardom. Vinney wished her well.

As for Denise, she would get through life easily enough – her kind always did. Lying there waiting for Nick, Vinney knew the nightmares of the past were no more. They had gone. The former panic-stricken Vinney Brandon did not exist in Vinney Wentworth, wife of Nick.

Her head turned at the sound of the door opening and then closing. Nick was striding across the room towards her in his bathrobe, sending her heart thudding against her ribs. At the bed he sloughed his robe and, as he slid into bed beside her, Vinney went into his arms to share with him all the wonder, all the promise, and all the frightening delight of love's fulfilment.

romance is beautiful!

and Harlequin Reader Service
is your passport to the
Heart of Harlequin

Harlequin is the world's leading publisher of romantic fiction novels. If you enjoy the mystery and adventure of romance, then you will want to keep up to date on all of our new monthly releases—eight brand new Romances and four Harlequin Presents.

If you are interested in catching up on exciting and valuable back issues, Harlequin Reader Service offers a wide choice of best-selling novels reissued for your reading enjoyment.

If you want a truly jumbo read and a money-saving value, the Harlequin Omnibus offers three intriguing novels under one cover by one of your favorite authors.

To find out more about Harlequin, the following information will be your passport to the Heart of Harlequin.

collection editions

Rare Vintage Romance
From Harlequin

The Harlequin Collection editions have been chosen
from our 400 through 899 series, and comprise some of
our earliest and most sought-after titles. Most of the
novels in this series have not been available since the
original publication and are available now in beautifully
redesigned covers.

When complete, these unique books will comprise the
finest collection of vintage romance novels available.
You will treasure reading and owning this delightful
library of beautiful love stories for many years to come.

For further information, turn to the back of this book and
return the INFORMATION PLEASE coupon.

the omnibus

A Great Idea! Three great romances by the same author, in one deluxe paperback volume.

A Great Value! Almost 600 pages of pure entertainment for only $1.95 per volume.

Essie Summers

Bride in Flight (#933)
...begins on the eve of Kirsty's wedding with the strange phone call that changed her life. Blindly, instinctively Kirsty ran — but even New Zealand wasn't far enough to avoid the complications that followed!

Postscript to Yesterday (#1119)
...Nicola was dirty, exasperated and a little bit frightened. She was in no shape after her amateur mechanics on the car to meet any man, let alone Forbes Westerfield. He was the man who had told her not to come.

Meet on My Ground (#1326)
...is the story of two people in love, separated by pride. Alastair Campbell had money and position — Sarah Macdonald was a girl with pride. But pride was no comfort to her at all after she'd let Alastair go!

Jean S. MacLeod

The Wolf of Heimra (#990)
...Fenella knew that in spite of her love for the island, she had no claim on Heimra yet — until an heir was born. These MacKails were so sure of themselves, they expected everything to come their way.

Summer Island (#1314)
...Cathie's return to Loch Arden was traumatic. She knew she was clinging to the past, refusing to let it go. But change was something you thought of happening in other places — never in your own beloved glen.

Slave of the Wind (#1339)
...Lesley's pleasure on homecoming and meeting the handsome stranger quickly changed to dismay when she discovered that he was Maxwell Croy — the man whose family once owned her home. And Maxwell was determined to get it back again.

Susan Barrie

Marry a Stranger (#1034)
...if she lived to be a hundred, Stacey knew she'd never be more violently in love than she was at this moment. But Edouard had told her bluntly that he would never fall in love with her!

Rose in the Bud (#1168)
...One thing Cathleen learned in Venice: it was highly important to be cautious when a man was a stranger and inhabited a world unfamiliar to her. The more charm he possessed, the more wary she should be!

The Marriage Wheel (#1311)
...Admittedly the job was unusual — lady chauffeur to Humphrey Lestrode; and admittedly Humphrey was high-handed and arrogant. Nevertheless Frederica was enjoying her work at Farthing Hall. Then along came her mother and beautiful sister, Rosaleen, to upset everything.

Violet Winspear

Beloved Tyrant (#1032)
...Monterey was a beautiful place to recuperate. Lyn's job was interesting. Everything, in fact, would have been perfect, Lyn Gilmore thought, if it hadn't been for the hateful Rick Corderas. He made her feel alive again!

Court of the Veils (#1267)
...In the lush plantation on the edge of the Sahara, Roslyn Brant tried very hard to remember her fiancé and her past. But the bitter, disillusioned Duane Hunter refused to believe that she ever was engaged to his cousin, Armand.

Palace of the Peacocks (#1318)
...Suddenly the island, this exotic place that so recently had given her sanctuary, seemed an unlucky place rather than a magical one. She must get away from the cold palace and its ghost — and especially from Ryk van Helden.

Isobel Chace

The Saffron Sky (#1250)
...set in a tiny village skirting the exotic Bangkok, Siam, the small, nervous Myfanwy Jones realizes her most cherished dream, adventure and romance in a far-off land. Two handsome men determine to marry her, but both have the same mysterious reason....

A Handful of Silver (#1306)
...in exciting Rio de Janeiro, city of endless beaches and skyscraper hotels, a battle of wits is waged between Madelaine Delahaye, Pilar Fernandez, the jealous fiancée of her childhood friend, and her handsome, treacherous cousin — Luis da Maestro....

The Damask Rose (#1334)
...Vicki Tremaine flies to the heady atmosphere of Damascus to meet Adam Templeton, fiancé of the rebellious Miriam. But alas, as time passes, Vicki only becomes more attracted to this young Englishman with the steel-like personality....

Jane Arbor

A Girl Named Smith (#1000)
...Mary Smith, a girl with a most uninspired name, a mouselike personality and a decidedly unglamorous appearance. That was how Mary saw herself. If this description had fitted, it would have been a great pleasure to the scheming Leonie Crispin and could have avoided a great deal of misunderstanding between Mary, Leonie and the handsomely attractive Clive Derwent....

Kingfisher Tide (#950)
...Rose Drake was about to realize her most cherished dream — to return to the small village of Maurinaire, France. The idea of managing her aunt's boutique shop produced grand illusions for Rose, but from the very day of her arrival, they were turned to dismay. The man responsible was the town's chief landowner and seigneur, a tyrant — living back in the days of feudalism....

The Cypress Garden (#1336)
...at the Villa Fontana in the Albano Hills in Italy, the young, pretty Alessandra Rhode is subjected to a cruel deception that creates enormous complications in her life. The two handsome brothers who participate pay dearly for their deceit — particularly, the one who falls in love....

Anne Weale

The Sea Waif (#1123)
...it couldn't be, could it? Sara Winchester, the beautiful and talented singer, stood motionless gazing at the painting in the gallery window. As she tried to focus through her tears, her thoughts went racing back to her sixteenth birthday, almost six years ago, and the first time she had set eyes on the sleek black-hulled sloop *Sea Wolf* and its owner, Jonathon "Joe" Logan....

The Feast of Sara (#1007)
...as Joceline read and re-read the almost desperate letter just received from cousin Camilla in France, pleading with Joceline to come and be with her, she sensed that something was terribly wrong. Immediately, she prepared to leave for France, filled with misgivings; afraid of learning the reason for her cousin's frantic plea....

Doctor in Malaya (#914)
...Andrea Fleming desperately wanted to accompany the film crew on the expedition, but Doctor James Ferguson was adamantly opposed, stating that if she went along, he would refuse to guide them. But Guy Ramsey had other ideas, and cunningly devised a scheme whereby Andrea would join them — in a manner the Doctor could do nothing about....

information please

**All the Exciting News from
Under the Harlequin Sun**

It costs you nothing to receive our news bulletins and
intriguing brochures. From our brand new releases to our
money-saving 3-in-1 omnibus and valuable best-selling
back titles, our information package is sure to be a hit.
Don't miss out on any of the exciting details. Send for
your Harlequin INFORMATION PLEASE package today.

MAIL COUPON TO ➡	Harlequin Reader Service, M.P.O. Box 707, Niagara Falls, New York 14302.
Canadian **SEND** Residents **TO:** ➡	Harlequin Reader Service, Stratford, Ont. N5A 6W4

Please send me the free Harlequin
Information Package

Name _____

Address _____

City _____

State/Prov. _____

Zip/Postal Code _____

MOR 2017